ATLANTA

HOMICIDE

BY

John C. Dalglish

2019

ATLANTA HOMICIDE

Sunday, December 17

Perimeter Loop
Atlanta, Georgia
7:45 p.m.

Monique Butler guided her blue Honda Civic off I-285, known locally as the perimeter loop, into the Collier Heights neighborhood. Next to Monique, her mother, Felicity Pope, stared out the passenger window at the chilly darkness. Typical for late December, the temperature varied between crisp but comfortable fifties during the day, to frosty thirties at night.

Felicity, dressed in a lavender print dress and a full-length black coat, had been quiet since they'd left the restaurant. Now in her sixties, Mom was less tolerant of the cold these days and regularly wore the heavy coat.

Monique touched her mother's arm. "You okay? You haven't said a word since we left the restaurant."

Her mother brushed back a long, curly strand of gray hair and smiled, her still perfect white teeth contrasting with the darkness of her skin. "I'm fine, dear. That was a wonderful dinner."

Monique returned the smile. "Did you enjoy seeing the Christmas lights?"

"Oh, yes. People do such a wonderful job on their homes, don't they?"

"They sure do. I'm glad we took time to drive around." Monique glanced over and nodded. Her mother's smile didn't come as readily as it used to, and their evening out had been an effort to remedy that. "We need to do this sort of thing more often."

Felicity nodded but to Monique's relief didn't take the opportunity to point out that her moving to Savannah was the reason these outings were so rare.

Focusing on the road, Monique steered along the eastern edge of the West Atlanta neighborhood. Listed in the National Register of Historic Places, Collier Heights held historical significance, which had much to do with why her mother had chosen to buy there. Felicity was proud to live near homes once owned by Martin Luther King, Sr. and Civil Rights Attorney Donald Hollowell.

Turning onto Renfro Drive, Monique slowed as they approached the small home shared by her mother and stepfather, Rodney Pope. His white Ford Fusion was in the carport, meaning he had returned from his evening walk at

4

the local park. Regardless of the weather, her stepfather took his nightly stroll.

She pulled into the driveway and parked. Her mother fished around in her purse for the house key then got out and approached the door. While her mother fiddled with the lock, Monique joined her on the stoop. The wind chilled them, and her mother seemed to be taking longer than usual to let them in.

"What's wrong, Mom?"

"The door won't budge."

"Is it unlocked?"

"Yes, I just can't move it."

Her mother stepped back, and Monique tried the door, turning the knob and pushing. It just barely moved. Putting her shoulder against the door, Monique leaned against it and shoved—this time opening it just a crack.

"There's something against the door."

Her mother's mood turned anxious. "A chair?"

"I'm not sure."

Monique steeled herself and shoved again, this time moving the door enough to look around the edge and see into the hallway. The only light came from the kitchen. It took her eyes a moment to adjust, and her mind another split second to comprehend what she was seeing.

"Dear Lord!"

She turned to her mother. "Get back in the car, Mom."

"Why? What is it?"

Monique pulled out her cellphone. "It's Rodney."

Her mother's eyes widened. "What about him? Is he okay?"

"I don't think so." She dialed 911. "Get out of the wind, Mom. I'm calling for help."

She watched her mother scurry back to the Honda as the dispatcher came on the line.

"Fulton County 9-1-1. What is your emergency?"

"My stepfather is down in our front hallway. I think he's been attacked."

"What is the address?"

"2905 Renfro Drive."

"What is your stepfather's name?"

"Rodney Pope."

"And what is your name?"

"Monique Butler."

"Okay. Stay with me. I have emergency personnel on the way. Is Mr. Pope conscious?"

The sight had already burned itself into her brain. "I don't think so. I don't know."

"Are you able to check for a pulse?"

"No. He's lying against the door."

"What about his chest? Can you see if it's rising and falling?"

"No! I don't know."

"Very well. Are you in a safe place?"

Monique went back to the car and got in next to her mother. "Yes. At least, I think so. I'm in my car with my mother."

"Good. Stay put until the officer approaches you, understand?"

"Yes."

She started the car and turned up the heat while they waited. Felicity was staring at Monique, but she avoided

6

meeting her mother's gaze. Surging up inside her was a trauma born out of the horror she had just witnessed. Afraid she couldn't hide her shock from her mom, Monique kept the phone pressed to her cheek and her eyes forward.

Despite the vehicle's heat, she shivered repeatedly. The cold of night had just taken on a whole new meaning.

Dale Creek Park
Collier Heights Neighborhood
West Atlanta
8:05 p.m.

Officer Tom Bradley sat in his cruiser with the overhead light on, filling out an accident report. He could go back to the precinct to do it, but chances were good he'd get very little done before having to return to his car.

"Dispatch to Unit 31."

His radio confirmed his suspicion. He picked up the mic. "Go for 31."

"Report of a man down in his home."

He laid his notepad on the passenger seat. "Address?"

"2905 Renfro Drive."

Probably less than a mile from his position. "What is his condition?"

"Unknown at this time."

"10-4. Unit 31 responding."

He hit his lights and sirens, and three minutes later, he pulled up in front of the house.

He grabbed his mic. "Dispatch, unit 31 is 10-97."

"Copy that, 31."

A woman got out of a blue Honda and approached his car. Bradley stepped out to meet her as she began yelling. Eyes wide with fear, she pointed over her shoulder at the front door. "He's in the front hallway!"

"Who is he, ma'am?"

"My stepfather."

Bradley tried to calm her. "Take a breath for me. What's your stepfather's name?"

The woman struggled to compose herself. "Rodney Pope."

"And what's your name?"

"Monique."

"Monique what?"

"Monique Butler."

Bradley started toward the door, the woman next to him. "Is there anyone else in the house?"

"I don't know."

Bradley caught sight of another person in the Honda. "Who is that?"

"My mother, Felicity Pope."

"Is she the man's wife?"

"Yes."

"Okay, listen to me." Bradley pointed toward the car. "I want you to sit with her in the car and not get out until I come for you. Understand?"

"Yes."

He waited for her to get in before pulling his flashlight and gun. Approaching the slightly ajar front door, he strained

8

to pick up any sound above the pounding of his heartbeat in his ears.

"Police! Anyone inside?"

He pushed on the door with the nose of his weapon, but it wouldn't budge. "Police!"

Sticking his flashlight through the opening then peering around the edge of the door, he looked down at the limp body of a man. The victim's back was against the door, his legs and feet stretched out away from him. "Sir! Can you hear me?"

No response, no movement.

Bradley considered forcing his way in but didn't want to move the victim any more than he already had. He stepped off the stoop and keyed his radio.

"Dispatch, this is 31."

"Go ahead, 31."

"I need medical personnel and a supervisor."

"Copy that. What is the situation?"

"I have one male down, possibly DOA. Attempting to make entrance to the home."

"10-4. I have back-up and medical being dispatched."

Bradley put away his gun and went to the Honda.

Monique Butler rolled down her window. "Is he dead?"

"I'm not sure, ma'am. Is there another way into the house?"

"Yes. Through the carport to the back door."

"Is it locked?"

"It should be."

"Do you have a key?"

Monique looked at her mother. "Mom?"

9

Mrs. Pope, her hands shaking noticeably, handed a key chain to her daughter. "It's the silver one."

Monique selected it and held the chain out the window.

Bradley took the keys. "Thank you. Stay here."

With his flashlight's help, he made his way past a white sedan in the small carport and into the backyard. Immediately to his left was a 9-pane entry door. The pane of glass next to the doorknob was broken out. He tried the knob and it turned.

Tucking the keys in his pocket, he drew his weapon again. When he pushed it open, the door made a grinding sound as it scraped across the shattered glass on the floor. Bradley stepped into a small kitchen.

Directly ahead, a short hallway led to the front door and the man on the floor. Bradley stepped gingerly around the glass, but with his senses heightened, his shoes against the tile still seemed to echo like a sonic boom.

"Anyone here? Police! Show yourself!"

Just silence.

He swept the room with his light then entered the hallway, moving quickly to where the victim lay. Blood seemed to be everywhere, from the floor to the walls, and up to the ceiling—the poor man had been brutally attacked.

Taking a quick look over his right shoulder, he cleared the living room then kneeled down and felt for a pulse on the man's neck. Nothing. Though still warm to the touch, Mr. Pope was clearly dead.

A staircase on Bradley's left went up to the second floor. He climbed the first few steps then paused. "Police! Anyone upstairs needs to show themselves now!"

The only answer was the sound of his own breathing—fast and shallow.

He made his way to the top and checked the first door on the right—a small bedroom. Quickly clearing it, he went to the next door on his right and entered another small bedroom, this one with a suitcase lying open on the bed. He cleared the room and moved on. In front of him was the bathroom, and after pulling back the shower curtain to satisfy himself no one was hiding there, he stepped back onto the landing.

The master bedroom faced out the front of the house. He approached, pushed the door open with his gun barrel, and scanned the room. The large bed was made and the curtains open. After a brief check of the walk-in closet, he was finally satisfied the house was clear.

Flashes of red and blue light streaked across the ceiling as sirens came to a halt out front. His back-up had arrived. He retreated down the steps and out the back door, being careful to disturb as little as possible. This little house on Renfro Drive was now a major crime scene.

Home of Detective Sean Sparks
Camden Vantage Apartments
Sweet Auburn Neighborhood
East of Downtown Atlanta
9:15 p.m.

The Sweet Auburn area of Atlanta had a rich history, including being the birthplace and tomb location of Martin

Luther King Jr. and the home of Detective Sean Sparks. Granted, his living there wasn't part of the area's significance, but the present-day synergy of historical significance and trendy, upscale amenities suited him well.

He gathered up two bowls of popcorn and headed back to the living room, where his longtime girlfriend Mariah Cooper, waited for him. She grinned up at him. "You look pretty good for a guy who's getting ready to turn forty."

With his close-cropped black curls and smooth brown skin, at first glance, he might pass for a man in his early twenties. However, the tinge of gray in his goatee would give away the truth—the Big Four-Oh was fast approaching.

He cast a wary eye at her. "No surprise party! You understand?"

She raised a hand to her chest. "Are you talking to me?"

He grunted. "You're darn right I'm talking to you."

She shook her head. "Don't worry. With your schedule, I could never plan one anyway."

He handed her a bowl of popcorn and sat down next to her on the couch. He lifted his arm for her, and she curled up against him, her black, shoulder-length curls tickling his face.

At just a shade over five feet tall, she easily fit into the crook of his arm, and her warmth filled him. Her brown eyes sparkled with the TV's reflection of her favorite Christmas movie—*It's a Wonderful Life.*

This was the third time they'd watched it in as many weeks, and Sean's attention was divided. His eyes were focused on the movie, but his ears and concentration were trained on the cellphone next to him. This night, he was the on-call detective.

He'd spent the last eight months in training with Lance Henderson, one of the best *ever* to carry the Atlanta PD homicide badge. Just this past week, Henderson had declared his protégé ready for his premier case as lead detective, and now, Sean was at the top of the assignment board. At thirty-nine, Sean wasn't exactly a rookie, but he still held the distinction of being the youngest and least experienced in Atlanta's Homicide Bureau.

Mariah giggled as George Bailey and Mary Hatch danced wildly back and forth, moving ever closer to the edge of the dance floor as it opened up above a pool. The couple was just pitching backward into the water when Sean's phone rang.

His adrenaline surged, and he spilled his popcorn reaching for his cell. "Hello?"

"Sparks?"

"Yes."

"This is Lieutenant Mitchell. I need you to respond to a scene."

"Very well." His pad had been next to his phone. "Address?"

"2905 Renfro Drive, Collier Heights. Single male has been found deceased. Patrol sergeant has requested a detective."

"I'll be on my way shortly."

"Good. Forensics has been dispatched."

"Copy that. The medical examiner?"

"Also notified. Get with me first thing in the morning for an update."

"Yes, ma'am."

"Oh, and Sparks…"

"Ma'am?"

"Not only are you the lead on this, but you're going solo. Detective Henderson has another case."

Sean swallowed hard, seeking to lubricate is suddenly dry throat. "I understand."

"Good. Talk soon."

The line went dead.

Mariah looked up at him. "You catch a case?"

He nodded. "Over in Collier Heights."

A mixture of pride and disappointment painted her face. Well aware of how much this meant to him, she was still sorry to have their movie night wrecked. "Congratulations."

"Thanks."

"Think you'll be long?"

"I have no way of knowing."

"Mom said she was going to do some gift wrapping tonight. That usually means she's up till midnight." She shrugged and set the popcorn bowl aside. "I guess I'll see if she wants any help."

Sean looked back at the movie. George Bailey was holding a white bathrobe, staring at a bush, and declaring, "A fella doesn't find himself in this situation every day."

At that moment, a car came around the corner, the driver bringing news that George's father was seriously ill. George Bailey's life would never be the same after that moment.

Sean felt exactly the same way just then.

Home of Rodney and Felicity Pope
2905 Renfro Drive NW
Collier Heights Neighborhood
West Atlanta
9:45 p.m.

Sean pulled up at the address to find the chaos he'd expected. The forensic techs moved back and forth from their van as they set up to process the scene, and at least four squad cars were parked haphazardly along the street, their lights supplying a cascade of endless red and blue streaks. The ambulance, no longer required, was just leaving.

He parked, drew in a steadying breath, and got out. The yellow crime tape, which stretched across the front of the yard and disappeared around the back of the property, vibrated in the breeze. Despite his jacket, the cold air chilled him, and he wondered if it was the temperature or his nerves that were causing him to shiver. Probably both.

Sean held his badge up as he approached so the duty officer, whose job it was to track all comings and goings, could check it.

The officer lifted the tape. "Evening, Detective."

"Evening. Who was first on scene?"

The patrolman turned and pointed at another uniformed officer who was leaning against one of the patrol cars.

"Tom Bradley."

"Thanks."

As he walked toward Bradley, Sean took note of the two cars parked inside the crime tape—a blue Honda in the driveway and a white Ford sedan in the carport.

Bradley held out his hand to Sean. "Officer Bradley."

They shook.

"Detective Sparks. Nice to meet you. You were first to get here?"

"Yes."

"Give me the rundown."

"9-1-1 came in about a man unresponsive in his home. I arrived and tried to make entrance, but the doorway was blocked by the victim. I was given the key to enter the back door but found a pane of glass had been broken out, and the door was unlocked. Once inside, I cleared the house then checked on the victim. He had no signs of life."

"Who is he?"

"Rodney Pope, age sixty-seven. Lived here with his wife."

"Who made the 9-1-1 call?"

"Monique Butler. She's the stepdaughter."

"Where is she?"

Bradley turned and gestured toward a house across the street. "She and her mother, who was the other person on sight when I arrived, are inside a neighbor's home."

"Who's the mother?"

"Felicity Hope, age sixty-one. She's the wife of the victim. She and Miss Butler came home to discover her husband down."

"Have we gotten a statement from either of them?"

"Not beyond what they said when I arrived."

"What time was that?"

"Ten minutes past eight."

Sean looked over at the house where the two women had taken refuge. "Okay, ask them down to the precinct. I'll speak with them after I get done here."

"Okay."

"But first, walk me through your initial movements."

Bradley put away his pad and started toward the front stoop. "After getting the basics from the stepdaughter, I secured them in her car then approached the front door. I attempted to push it open but was met with resistance."

"Was it open?"

"Yes, about six inches or so."

Sean nodded. "Okay, go on."

"When I couldn't get it to budge, I managed to peer around the corner and see the victim prone on the floor. Not wanting to move him, I returned to the car where the ladies were and secured keys to the back door." Bradley headed toward the carport, still speaking, as Sean trailed him. "I reached the back door and found the broken window. The door was unlocked."

As they reached the back door, Sean pulled on latex gloves. Bradley already had some on and pushed the door open for them to enter. Sean kneeled and examined the glass, which most notably was on the kitchen floor, meaning it had been broken from the outside.

He stood and followed Bradley into the hallway, steeling himself for his first glimpse of the victim.

Bradley finished his narration. "As I came inside, I cleared the kitchen then made my way down the hallway to where I found the victim."

ATLANTA HOMICIDE

The sight of all the blood hit Sean like a punch in the gut. Spatter covered every surface—from the floor to the ceiling. Staring down at Mr. Pope, Sean paused to draw in a couple deep breaths. Without the benefit of identification, it would be nearly impossible to know who the man was. Someone had beaten him merciless about the head and face.

Sean glanced over at the officer. "You find a weapon?"

Bradley shook his head. "Not yet, but we haven't done a full search. We were waiting for you and forensics."

Sean nodded. Whatever had been used on this poor man, it had been targeted almost exclusively at his head. Someone had wanted to make sure Mr. Pope did not survive the attack. A blood smear on the front door indicated that the victim had slid to the floor and remained where he was.

Bloody shoeprints led down the hall toward the kitchen, but at first glance, they appeared badly smeared and probably wouldn't be much help. Sean found a gap in the blood to place his foot and support his weight without disturbing anything, then leaned over the body. "He hasn't been moved, right?"

"Correct. Just the amount it took to see through the crack in the door."

A glimmer on the floor near the hallway baseboard caught Sean's eye—a set of keys. "You see those?"

Bradley peered at them. "I hadn't till now."

"So, those aren't the ones you were given?"

Bradley tapped his pocket. "No. I still have them."

"Then those may belong to the victim. Looks like he might have been attacked as soon as he came through the door."

Sean reached around Pope's contorted lower body and found a wallet in the man's back pocket. Sean extracted it, stood up, and pulled the driver's license. The stated age was sixty-seven, but the photo revealed bright-green eyes and a full head of hair that gave Pope a more youthful look.

Sean checked the wallet's contents. "Cards are here; so is some cash."

He glanced over into the living room where he spotted a TV and a DVD player, both items a burglar would have taken. Robbery didn't seem a likely motive here, but only after a full accounting of the home's contents by Mrs. Pope, would he be able to rule out that motive completely.

A member of the crime scene investigation team came in. "Can we start processing, Detective?"

Sean nodded. "Yes. You have an evidence bag on you?"

The female tech produced one, and Sean dropped the wallet into it. He pointed at the footprints. "It looks like we may have some shoe impressions, probably from our killer or killers."

"I see that. We'll pay special attention to them."

Sean gestured at the keys on the floor. "Make sure those aren't missed, please."

"Yes, sir."

"But first, the glass on the kitchen floor needs photographed and bagged."

The tech nodded. "On it."

"Thank you." Sean looked at Bradley. "Did you determine who the vehicles in the driveway belong to?"

Bradley nodded. "The white sedan belonged to the victim, and the Honda is the stepdaughter's."

19

"Do you know if the neighborhood canvass has started?"

"Affirmative. My supervisor, Sergeant Young, is heading it up."

"Okay, go ahead and have our witnesses taken downtown."

"Will do."

"Oh, but before putting them in an interview room, have a forensic tech check them for blood with an alternate light source."

"Very well."

"Then stay with them until I get there."

"Yes, sir."

"By the way…"

Bradley hesitated. "Sir?"

"Good thinking about not moving the body during entry."

"Thanks."

As Bradley left, Sean moved into the living room, scanning the floor with his flashlight despite the glow cast by a nearby floor lamp. From his cursory exam, the crime seemed mostly to be contained to the hallway. The furniture was nice but not lavish, and the house appeared in overall good order—no signs of a struggle—further suggesting the attack began as soon as Mr. Pope entered the house.

In addition, a bit of spatter near the archway entrance to the foyer was the only blood in the living room. No bloody footprints marred the low-pile carpeting—at least, none that were visible to the naked eye.

The killer didn't come through here after the attack; that's for sure.

A luminol treatment would confirm his impression.

20

The living room ran parallel to the hallway, back toward a small dining room, and then around to a separate entrance to the kitchen. Everything was tidy in the dining room, and no food or dishes remained from an evening meal. More importantly, there was still no murder weapon.

Sean reached the back door again as the rest of the crime scene techs entered. They spread out like worker bees and began an assortment of tasks, including photographing everything, dusting for prints, and getting biological samples.

Sean stepped back out into the night, letting his flashlight play across the back yard. A single gate gave access through the fence into the alley behind the property. He made his way to it and checked for a lock but found none. He opened the gate and let his light play on the dirt in the alley.

Was that a footprint?

He returned to the kitchen and found the tech who had secured the wallet. "Excuse me?"

"Sir?"

"Come with me, will you?"

The tech followed Sean to the alley.

Sean let his light fall on the smudge in the dirt. "That look like a print to you?"

The tech added the illumination from her light to his. "Could be."

Sean scanned the alley. The only purpose for the dark area seemed to be storing the numerous garbage cans lined up behind the homes. The murder weapon could well be in one of them. "I'm going to have the alley blocked off at both ends and searched. Be sure to get this print."

"Yes, sir."

They headed back to the house. Sean secured a yellow, numbered triangle from the tech then returned to the back gate to place it by the print to keep others from disturbing the possible evidence.

Satisfied it was protected, Sean crossed the yard to the carport. He glanced at his watch then rested his hand on the hood. It had been roughly two hours since the call came in, so he wasn't surprised the metal was cool to the touch.

He headed back up front and went over to the entry log officer.

"Can you radio Sergeant Young?"

"Sure."

"Good. Get him for me."

Sergeant Young, you copy?"

"Go for Young."

"I have Detective Sparks here. He wants to talk to you." The officer handed his radio to Sean.

"Sergeant Young?"

"Yes."

"Can you have your officers doing the neighborhood canvass request permission from the homeowners to search their backyards?"

"Sure. What are they looking for?"

"Something bloody."

A brief hesitation. "Copy that."

"Thanks. Sparks out."

Sean handed the radio back. "Get two officers, have them park their patrol cars at either end of the alley behind the house then conduct a search for evidence—especially inside garbage cans."

"Yes, sir."

"Thanks."

"Hey, Detective Sparks."

Sean turned to see Medical Examiner Ryan Carter coming toward him. "Hey, Doc."

"Henderson here with you?"

Sean shook his head.

The round-faced, barrel-chested Carter smiled broadly. "You running lead on this one?"

Sean smirked. "Lead and solo!"

Carter's thick brows spiked. "Whoa! Jumping in with both feet, I guess."

"Just doing what the boss tells me."

"Always a wise decision. Where's our vic?"

"This way."

Sean led Carter through the carport and the back door, where a tech was just finishing bagging the glass shards. Forensics had set up portable lights on the hallway, illuminating the bloody scene. Carter snapped on his pair of latex gloves and surveyed the carnage. "Wow. Someone did a number on this poor fella."

"You can say that again."

Carter pointed upward. "There's as much blood up there as on the walls. You find a weapon?"

"No."

"Just quickly looking at the wounds and the blood, I'd bet this was a long object rather than something short."

"You mean a stick rather than a rock?"

"In simple terms, yes. The object seemed to be swinging up near the ceiling."

Carter kneeled next to the body. "All the photos taken?"

"I believe so."

The medical examiner lifted one of the victim's arms and moved a finger then extracted a scalpel and thermometer from his bag. Lifting Rodney Pope's shirt, Carter made a small incision in the abdomen then inserted the thermometer into the liver. After a couple moments, he extracted the instrument and stared at the number.

"Roughly speaking, TOD would be about two hours ago and probably no longer than three. Rigor is in the very early stages, so say…" He glanced at his watch. "Seven or seven-thirty, thereabouts."

Sean nodded. "When do you think you'll do the autopsy?"

"Probably not until late tomorrow. I'll let you know."

"Thanks, Doc. I'll leave you to it."

Sean returned to the carport. Still with his gloves on, he opened the door of the white sedan and examined the interior. Like the house, it was tidy. He checked the center compartment, glove box, and under the seat for a weapon but came up empty. He then popped the trunk and got out to check there but still found nothing other than a spare tire.

With no temperature reference on the car, Sean was left with several questions.

Did Mr. Pope get a ride home? Or did he drive himself? And was he alone when he went inside?

Sean closed the trunk and moved on to the Honda. This vehicle was less neat; in fact, it was pretty messy. Still, Sean found no weapons and no blood.

He returned to the back gate where the lead tech was photographing the footprint. "I need the vehicles processed."

The tech looked up. "You want them impounded?"

"Yeah. Take them both downtown and go over them with a fine-tooth comb."

"You're the boss."

Odd as it felt, the tech was right. On this one, he was in charge. He went back to his car.

The attack *felt* as if it was targeted. *But why would someone want Rodney Pope dead?*

Sean needed to know a lot more about his victim if he was going to answer that question.

The two women were waiting for him at the station. Maybe they could answer some of his questions.

Hopefully, someone could!

ATLANTA HOMICIDE

Monday, December 18

Atlanta Police Headquarters
Homicide Division
226 Peachtree Street SW
Downtown Atlanta
12:30 a.m.

Police Headquarters was a four-story, red brick structure with floor-to-ceiling windows, located in the southern part of downtown. With the adjacent city detention center to the southwest and the city courthouse on the southeast, the three buildings made up the triangle of the Atlanta justice system.

A half mile to the east was the Georgia State Capitol building, and north of that, the Atlanta underground. Also nearby, sat the Mercedes-Benz stadium, so to say the area was busy would be an understatement, but things were relatively quiet at twelve-thirty in the morning.

Sean stopped briefly at his desk to pick up a recorder and run a driver's license check on both women, then headed for the interview suites.

Officer Bradley sat in a chair in the hallway and looked up as Sean approached.

"They're in room three."

"Okay. The scan?"

"Came back clean—no traces. We also got fingerprints from both."

"Excellent. I'll take it from here. Thanks."

27

"No problem."

Sean pushed the door to room three open. The two women, sitting close together, looked up with a start.

He shut the door behind him. "Sorry, didn't mean to startle you."

Monique shook her head. "No, it's fine." Her hands encircled her mother's. "We were just saying a few prayers."

"I can come back if you like."

"No. It's been a long night already. We want to get whatever you need over with."

"Of course, and I appreciate your patience."

A small table divided the women from two empty chairs. Sean sat in one and placed a digital recorder on the table.

"I hope you don't mind, but I'll be recording our conversation."

Miss Butler nodded. "We understand."

While Sean laid out a pad and pen on the desk, he examined the women in front of him.

Monique Butler sat composed in beige slacks and a white top, her black braids pulled into a loose ponytail. Her legs were crossed at the ankles and her shoulders straight, but the arch of her eyebrows and tightness around her mouth spoke to an underlying tension, which was understandable considering the events of that evening. Her dark-brown eyes seemingly took in everything around her at once. Her license said she was forty-one.

Felicity Pope had gray curls that fell past her shoulders. She held a thick black coat so tight to her chest that her light-brown skin had turned white around her knuckles. Her stare from bloodshot eyes was one of shock—vacant and distant.

"I'm very sorry for your loss."

Felicity didn't move.

Monique dipped her head slightly. "Thank you."

Sean turned on the recorder. "I'm Detective Sean Sparks. It's Monday, December eighteenth, and the time is twelve forty-three a.m. With me are Felicity Pope and Monique Butler. This interview is in connection with the death of Rodney Pope." He looked up at the women. "Miss Butler, you're here voluntarily, correct?"

"Yes."

"And Mrs. Pope, you're here voluntarily also, correct?"

Felicity nodded weakly.

Sean forced a sympathetic smile. "I need you to say yes aloud, please."

"Oh…yes."

"Thank you. Now, starting with the time you arrived home, please tell me what happened."

Monique spoke up immediately. "We pulled into the driveway just before eight, I believe. Mom got out first and went to the front door. I came up behind her and waited, but she didn't go inside. When I asked her what the problem was, she said the door was jammed."

Sean was watching Felicity while her daughter spoke. "Was the door unlocked, Mrs. Pope?"

"Yes."

Sean nodded, and Monique continued.

"So, I stepped around her and tried to get it open myself. When it didn't give at all, I leaned against it and shoved. That opened it a crack. I was able to look around the edge of the door, and that's when I…" She squeezed her mother's hand. "That's when we found him."

"What did you do then?"

"Well, I didn't want Mom to see such a terrible sight, so I told her to get back in the car. Then I called 9-1-1."

Sean made a note. "Now, if you would, start at the beginning of your day and tell me everything you did."

Monique's face darkened. "Everything?"

"Please."

"I don't understand. Why?"

Sean had to walk a fine line between being understanding of their grief and getting the information he needed for the investigation. Days from now, these same women would want answers as to why their loved one was killed, and what they said tonight could go a long way toward answering those questions.

"Knowing how your day unfolded can be very important in understanding the last hours of Mr. Pope's life. I wouldn't put you through this if it wasn't critically important."

While Monique seemed pacified, Felicity remained stoic, disconnected.

Monique shifted in her seat. "Well, I've been visiting from Savannah, where I live, and staying with my mother since Friday. We got up around eight or so this morning, made coffee, and chatted until around ten."

Sean held up a hand. "Was Mr. Pope with you?"

"No. He slept in."

"Okay."

"So, we dressed and went shopping at Atlantic Station. We had lunch at the Atlantic Grill in the mall then returned home around two."

"Was Mr. Pope at home when you returned?"

She nodded. "Yes. He was watching TV."

"Did everything seem normal?"

"Yes."

"Okay, go ahead."

Monique shifted again. "Anyway, I went on my laptop for a while, and Mom took a nap. About six, Rodney left for his usual walk."

"His usual walk?"

"Yes. He drives to Scott Park and then takes a walk."

The park didn't ring a bell with Sean, so he made a note. "He does this *every* night?"

"That's right, rain or shine."

"And always the same place?"

Monique looked at her mother. "Always the same, right, Mom?"

Felicity, though she didn't appear to be tuned in, nodded.

Monique continued. "Anyway, not long after he left, Mom and I went out for dinner."

"Where did you go?"

"The Colonnade."

Sean *did* know that place; in fact, everyone in Atlanta was familiar with it. The restaurant had been around since the 1920's. "Did you go anywhere else?"

Monique shook her head. "Not specifically. After dinner, we drove through some neighborhoods to look at Christmas lights then came home, which was when…"

"Right." Sean looked at Felicity. "Mrs. Pope?"

The woman slowly lifted her eyes to meet his. "Yes?"

"Can you think of anyone who would want to hurt your husband?"

Her eyes widened. "No…no one."

"What did your husband do for a living?"

"He's retired now, but he worked at Home Depot for over ten years. Before that, he was in the Coast Guard."

"How long had you and Mr. Pope been married?"

"Seven…" The words seemed to stick in her throat. Monique finished. "Seven years."

Sean looked at some of his notes from the scene. "What about other family? Did Mr. Pope have anyone else we should speak to?"

Monique dug around in her purse. "He has one daughter from his first marriage who lives in Midtown." She pulled out an address book and opened it. "Her name is Janine Evans."

Sean wrote down the daughter's name along with the number Monique read off.

"Has anyone called her?"

"Neither of us has."

"Do you know if Miss Evans had a good relationship with her father?"

"As far as I know, they were close."

"Okay. What about his first wife?"

Monique put away the address book. "She passed away twenty years ago."

"I see." Sean looked at his watch. "Do you ladies have a place to stay? You won't be allowed back in the house."

"I'll get Mom and me a hotel room."

"Good. Please let me know where you are. I won't keep you any longer, and we'll talk again tomorrow."

"Very well." Monique stood and touched her mother's shoulder. "Come on, Mom. We need to get you somewhere to rest."

Felicity Pope struggled to her feet and followed her daughter out of the room. Sean turned off the recorder. His next task would be much tougher than this interview—notifying Mr. Pope's other daughter.

Home of Janine Evans
Myrtle Street NE
Midtown Atlanta
5:30 a.m.

Midtown, a subdivision located on the east side of the city, was especially known for being the location of the Margaret Mitchell House, where the famous author had written most of *Gone with the Wind*. Before going to Miss Evans's home, Sean had stopped by the crime scene to check on how things were progressing with the evidence gathering. Regardless of the side trip, he still arrived on Myrtle Street long before the sun had cracked the eastern sky.

Janine Evans lived in a small, single-story home, and typical of the area, it sat up on a rise and away from street level. The entrance to the home was up two sets of concrete stairs leading from the sidewalk. The porch light was on, but the remainder of the house was dark.

Sean knocked on the wood door and waited as the wind blew leaves around his feet. He was forced to pull his jacket tighter around him as a defense against the cold. When no one came, he knocked again, this time more forcefully.

Still no answer.

He returned to his car, got out his phone, and dialed the number for Miss Evans. It rang several times before a woman picked up.

"Hello?"

"Janine Evans?"

"Yes. Who's this?"

"My name is Detective Sparks. I'm with the Atlanta Police Department."

"Hello, Detective. Is there something wrong?"

"I'm outside your home. Can you come to the door?"

"No, I'm sorry. I'm at work. What's this about, Detective?"

Sean steeled himself. He preferred to do this sort of thing in person, but...

"It's about your father, Rodney Pope."

"My Dad? What about him?"

"I'm afraid he's passed away."

The line went silent. Sean waited nearly a minute.

"Miss Evans?"

"I'm...I'm here." Her voice trembled. "What happened?"

"We believe he was attacked shortly after arriving home last night."

"Attacked!"

"Yes, ma'am. Your father was murdered."

Sobs reverberated through the phone. Sean paused, waiting for the woman to gather herself.

"Miss Evans?"

"Yes?"

"I know you're at work. May I ask where that is?"

"I'm a nurse at Northside Hospital."

Sean had been there many times. Located where the northbound Harvey Mathis Parkway intersected the Perimeter Loop, even without traffic, it was at least thirty minutes away.

"I need to meet with you, Miss Evans. Would you like me to come there?"

"No. I need to get someone to cover, and I'll head home."

"How long will that be?"

"I can't say exactly."

"Can I ask you to call me when you feel up to talking? I'll come back to your home."

"Of course."

"Does my number show on your phone?"

A brief hesitation. "Yes."

"I'm very sorry for your loss."

"I need to go."

The line went dead. Sean tossed his phone on the seat and started the car. In the early light of morning, he turned his car around and headed back to the precinct. Lieutenant Mitchell, if she stayed true to form, would be in her office by six a.m.

Might as well bring her up to speed, though there wasn't much to tell yet.

ATLANTA HOMICIDE

Office of Lieutenant Shannon Mitchell
Atlanta Police Headquarters
Homicide Division
226 Peachtree Street SW
Downtown Atlanta
6:45 a.m.

With her blonde hair and blue eyes, a brilliant smile, and a physique kept trim through regular exercise, Lieutenant Shannon Mitchell appeared better suited for the fashion runway than the front office of the Atlanta major crimes division, but it only took a brief conversation with her to dispel any misconceptions about her abilities as a cop. She knew her stuff, and if you didn't, it wouldn't be long before she exposed you. That meant being prepared to brief her.

On the other hand, she was fair to a fault, and nothing meant more to her than the well-being of her detectives. She would take on anyone in the department, all the way up to and including the chief, if she thought her detectives were being treated improperly. That trait had earned her the undying devotion of the men and women under her.

Sean tapped on the door frame. "Lieutenant?"

Mitchell looked up. "Sean, come in. Shut the door."

He did then took a seat opposite his boss. "Had a moment, so I wanted to bring you up to speed."

She laid down her pen and leaned back in her chair. "Perfect. What have you got?"

"Victim is Rodney Pope, age sixty-seven. He was found in the entryway to his home and appeared to have been attacked shortly after arriving. Coroner put the initial TOD at between seven and eight last night. While not official, he also suggested blunt force trauma as the likely cause of death."

Mitchell crossed her arms over her chest. "Find a weapon?"

"Not yet. I'm having the garbage cans along the alley behind the home searched. I also asked that the canvass officers get permission to search the backyards of the homes around the Pope residence. I thought our perp might have tossed the weapon while leaving the scene."

Mitchell nodded. "I like it."

I like it. Those three words were as close to a gold star as you could get from Mitchell. He shrugged. "As of yet, nothing has been found."

"What about the canvass itself? Did it turn up anything?"

"I'm waiting for the reports now."

"Got any leads?"

"Nothing I can latch on to and run with. I've already met with the stepdaughter and the wife of the victim. I'm also planning to meet with Mr. Pope's biological daughter later this morning."

"What about motive?"

"I still have to bring the wife over to the home to make sure we can rule out robbery, but my gut says this was a targeted attack. Common items normally taken were left behind."

"Sounds good. Anything you need from me?"

"Not at the moment."

"Let me know if you do." She leaned forward and picked up her pen.

Sean stood. "Yes, ma'am."

He went back out to his desk and dropped into his chair. The clock on the squad room wall read 7:00 a.m. Mariah would be getting ready for work. He dialed her number.

"Hello?"

"Hey, babe. It's me."

"Morning, Sean. How's it going? Catch the bad guy yet?"

He smiled. "Not yet. How did the gift wrapping go?"

"Fine. Mom hadn't wrapped your gift yet, so I got to see what it was."

"And?"

"And what?"

"Aren't you going to tell me what she got me?"

"You're the detective. You figure it out."

He laughed. "But what if I don't like it?"

"You'll like it—trust me."

"I do."

"Will I see you later?"

"No way for me to know right now. I'll touch base later."

She groaned. "Okay. Love you."

"Love you more."

"Not possible."

The line went dead. Sean looked up as a uniformed officer stopped next to his desk.

"Detective Sparks?"

"Yeah?"

The officer laid a thick manila envelope on Sean's desk. "Canvass reports."

"Great. Thanks."

Sean opened the flap and slid an inch-thick batch of papers out onto his desk. He stared at the pile, reached

John C. Dalglish

blindly for his coffee cup, and took a sip. He grimaced and swallowed the ice-cold brew. With a sigh, he pushed himself back from his desk, got up, and headed over to the coffee machine.

Lance Henderson was filling his own cup. "Hey, Rook."

Despite Sean's years on the force, Henderson measured everyone by how long they had been a homicide detective. That made Sean a rookie.

"Hi, Lance."

"I heard you got your first case."

"You heard right. Expected to be working it with you, but Mitchell said no. What's on your plate?"

"Double murder up in Bankhead."

Sean was familiar with the neighborhood, northwest of downtown. "Sounds brutal."

"Appears to be the result of a love triangle. What about yours?"

Sean took the coffee pot from Henderson and filled his cup. "Elderly man killed in his front hallway. Bloody scene."

"Any leads?"

"Not yet."

Henderson lifted his cup in a mock toast. "Welcome to the big time, Rook."

Sean smirked. "Thanks."

****

Sean refilled his cup twice more in the three hours it took him to work his way through the neighborhood canvass interviews. Only one stood out as having something useful.

39

The woman who lived two doors down on the same side of the street as the Pope residence had heard a commotion in the alley behind her home.

He was about to pick up his phone to make an appointment when it rang.

"Homicide—Detective Sparks."

"Yes, Detective, this is Janine Evans."

"Oh, hi. Thanks for calling. Are you available for me to come over?"

"I just got home. I'd like some time first, if that's okay."

"Of course. What time would be good?"

"Twelve-thirty."

Sean would have preferred much sooner, but he saw no point in pressing the woman.

"That's fine. I'll see you then."

"Okay."

The line went dead.

Sean glanced at the number of his witness and dialed.

After multiple rings, someone picked up. "Hello?"

"Mrs. Collins?"

"Yes."

"This is Detective Sparks with the Atlanta police department."

"Oh, hello, Detective. How can I help you?"

"I was wondering if I might drop by and speak with you."

"Is this about that nasty business at the Popes'?"

Sean could almost see the curl in the woman's lip. "Yes, ma'am."

"Awful thing, that."

"Yes, ma'am."

"Person's not even safe in their home anymore."

"It seems that way sometimes, ma'am."

Like a flipped switch, her tone brightened. "You come on over. I'd be happy to chat with you."

"Very well, ma'am. I'll see you soon."

"Okay."

He hung up and dialed Monique Butler's cellphone. The call went to voicemail.

This is Monique. Sorry to miss your call. Leave me a message and I call you back, I promise.

The tone sounded.

"Miss Butler, this is Detective Sparks. Please call me as soon as possible."

He hung up and looked at his watch. With more than two hours to kill before going to Janine Evans's place, he hoped to visit with Mrs. Collins *and* walk the crime scene with Felicity Pope. Lunch would have to be something from a drive-thru.

Home of Opal Collins
2901 Renfro Drive NW
Collier Heights Neighborhood
West Atlanta
10:25 a.m.

Just two doors east of the Pope residence sat a nearly identical house—the most noticeable difference being the white, decorative metal bars over the front door and windows. Encircled by tall trees, the home's landscape was covered with leaves, which seemed to cling desperately to the lawn in a struggle against the cold wind's effort to blow them away.

From where Sean parked on the street, he could see the Atlanta PD patrol car in front of the Pope home, keeping vigil and maintaining the security of his crime scene. Yellow crime tape shimmered in the wind, contrasting with the patrol car's midnight-blue body and red-striped sides.

Sean stepped out into the bright sun, pulled his jacket tight against the wind, and walked up on the small stoop. Just moments after he rang the bell, the front door swung wide, and a woman Sean guessed to be in her late seventies or early eighties stared at him through the bars. Even with her wispy gray hair pulled up on top of her head, she couldn't have stood more than four feet six or seven.

She gazed at him with lively steel-blue eyes and smiled. "You must be the detective?"

"Yes, ma'am. We spoke on the phone."

She grunted. "I remember! I'm old—not daft."

Sean smiled. "I didn't mean to suggest..."

"Of course you didn't." She grinned back at him and unlocked the metal door. "Please come in."

Sean followed her inside, immediately recognizing the layout as matching the Pope home. Of course, no blood spattered the walls, and instead of death, he smelled fresh coffee.

"I'm Opal Collins, but since you're a detective, I'm guessing you already knew that."

Sean liked this lady. "Yes, I had come to that conclusion."

"I just made some coffee. Interested?"

"Yes, please."

Opal nodded. "Good. Follow me."

She led him down the short hallway to the kitchen and pointed at a small table with just two chairs. "Make yourself comfortable."

Sean pulled out the closest chair and sat. Opal, whose movements were surprisingly nimble for someone her age, quickly set a cup of steaming coffee in front of him.

"Cream or sugar?"

He shook his head. "No, thank you."

She lowered herself into the chair opposite him and dumped some non-dairy creamer into her cup. While she stirred her coffee, Sean sipped the liquid warmth. His reaction must have shown on his face.

Opal smirked. "Strong, huh?"

He nodded. "Stronger than I'm used to."

"You like it?"

"I do. Beats the heck out of the watered-down stuff they make at the precinct."

She beamed. "I've been making it the same way for twenty years. My husband, God rest his soul, loved his coffee strong. I use to say it would stand on its own without a mug. Anyway, we bought one of those drip coffeemakers that had a strong brew button on it. He wasn't satisfied."

"What did you do?"

"I started taking the finished pot and running it immediately through the grinds a second time. He loved it— and since I loved him, I learned to like my coffee that way."

"I would have thought it would be bitter."

Opal shook her head. "Nope. Secret is to do it right away." She took a large swallow from her cup, set it down, then fixed him with a serious look. "Anyway, you didn't come here to discuss coffee. I'm no detective, but I know that much. What can I help you with?"

Sean set his cup down and extracted his notepad. "You told one of our officers that something unusual occurred around the time Mr. Pope was killed."

"That's correct. It was just after seven on Sunday night. I know the time because *60 Minutes* had just started."

"You heard something, I gather?"

Opal pointed at the next room. "I was sitting right there when a commotion caught my attention."

In the Pope house, it was the dining room, but Opal had it set up as a TV room.

Sean glanced at the window that looked out on the back yard. "It must have been loud."

"It was, but I had the window open, as well."

"Open?"

"Sure—I love the fresh air. Course, it was a little chilly, so it was only cracked."

To Sean, the temperature had been more than just chilly that night, but the longer he spoke with Mrs. Opal Collins, the less surprised he was by what she said. "Is the alley normally pretty quiet?"

"Yes. Just people putting their trash out, and of course, the trucks on trash day."

"So, what did you do?"

"I stood and looked out the back window toward the alley."

Sean stood and went over to the window, pulling the drape back so he could see what Opal's view of the alley was. Her back fence line was clear of obstruction. Sean's hopes surged. "Did you get a look at who was out there?"

"Nope. It had already gotten dark."

"What did the disturbance sound like?"

"As if someone had run into a trash can and knocked it over. Then footsteps running away."

"Could you tell how many people were out there?"

"Nope."

Sean's optimism waned. "Is there anything else you may have noticed that evening?"

"Nope. That was it—until sirens started wailing about an hour later."

Sean considered how Opal's information jived with the timeline he'd been working with. Doc Carter's initial assessment now appeared even stronger when matched to the time Opal reported hearing noises. Her statement also gave Sean the likely path of escape for the killer or killers.

He returned to the table. "Thank you for your time."

"Got nothing but."

He smiled and downed the rest of his coffee. "You've been very helpful."

"Want a refill?"

He was considering it when his phone rang. Recognizing the number as Monique Butler's, he shook his head. "No, thank you. I need to take this call, so I'll let myself out."

"Suit yourself."

He smiled and mouthed goodbye, while hitting the answer button. "Detective Sparks."

"Yes, Detective. This is Monique Butler returning your call."

He made it down the hallway and stepped outside. "Thank you for getting back to me. Is your mother with you?"

"She is."

"How's she holding up?"

Monique sighed. "About as well as one could hope, I think."

"I'm glad to hear that. Unfortunately, I need to ask something of her. It won't be easy, but it's very important."

"What is it?"

"Do you think she could go through the house with me?"

A pause. "Why is this important?"

"One of the key things I need to determine in order to catch your father's killer is motive—why someone wanted him dead. By checking to see if anything is missing, your mom can help me determine whether robbery played a part in the events leading up to Mr. Pope's death."

"Uh…" A long silence followed.

Sean hated putting people through things like this, but it was a necessary evil. "Mr. Pope's body is not in the house any longer, of course, but the scene hasn't been cleaned up yet."

"Okay…hold on."

Something muffled the phone so Sean couldn't make out the exact conversation, but Monique came back on shortly.

"Detective?"

"Yes."

"My mom seems to feel she's strong enough to do it. I assume I can help her with this?"

46

"Of course. I appreciate it very much."

"When?"

"As soon as you can would be great."

"Thirty minutes okay?"

"Perfect. I'll see you then."

He hung up and looked at the time. He should be able to get the search done and still be on time for his meeting with Janine Evans. Despite the cold, he walked the two doors down to the Pope residence.

Home of Rodney and Felicity Pope
2905 Renfro Drive NW
Collier Heights Neighborhood
West Atlanta
11:30 a.m.

Monique Butler and Felicity Pope showed up right on time, and not surprisingly, wearing the same clothes from the night before. Monique greeted Sean first and was clearly the more refreshed of the two women. Rodney Pope's wife didn't appear to have slept at all since she'd learned of her husband's death.

Sean searched Felicity Pope's eyes. "Are you sure you're up to this?"

A weak nod. "I just want to get it over with."

"Very well. We're going to enter through the back door, and please take as much time as you need. Scan each room for anything you think is moved or missing."

"Okay."

"We'll go from the kitchen, into the dining room, then the living room, and lastly, into the hallway. From there, we'll go upstairs."

Despite her weariness, her demeanor appeared resolute. "I understand."

"I'm right here, Mom." Monique took her mother's hand. "Detective, will we be able to get a change of clothes, maybe our makeup?"

Sean nodded. "Yes, but I'll have to note anything you remove."

"How long before we can have the house cleaned and get back inside?"

"I can't say for sure. Hopefully, just a few days."

Though Monique appeared frustrated, she didn't look surprised. "Ready, Mom?"

"Yes."

As if he was the grand marshal of a kind of morbid parade, Sean led the two women to the back of the house and into the kitchen. The coppery odor of dried blood washed over them as they entered, and Mrs. Pope reacted by swaying on her feet, then grabbing at the door frame to keep from falling backward. Monique reached out to steady her mother.

When Mrs. Pope had poised herself, and without further prompting, she began to scan the kitchen. Black fingerprint powder residue was everywhere, but if it bothered her, she didn't let on. Whether out of self-preservation or sheer force of will, Felicity Pope moved forward.

She shook her head. "Nothing."

She entered the dining room, circled around the table, and shook her head again. "Nothing."

As she entered the living room, her gaze flicked briefly to the hall, but then she looked quickly away. Monique stayed right next to her mother, but they didn't speak.

Suddenly, Pope stopped. "My money."

Sean's heart rate instantly doubled. "Your money?"

The woman moved over to the mantel on the far wall and reached for something.

"Don't!"

She froze.

"I'm sorry; I didn't mean to startle you." Sean went over to her. "I should have told you outside that we don't want to touch anything if we can help it."

Sitting at one end of the small mantel was a plastic mug bearing the insignia of *Harrah's Casino*. The mug looked like one you got to keep if you ordered a piña colada. He hadn't noticed it the previous night. "You kept money in that?"

"Yes. My fun money for when I went to the casino."

Sean pulled on a pair of latex gloves he'd brought with him for just such a reason. He tilted the white plastic cup and looked inside. "It's empty. How much was in here?"

"Over three hundred dollars. It was my winnings from the last time I went."

The cup hadn't been dusted for prints. He would need to bag it and take it in.

"My laptop!" Monique was pointing. "It's gone."

Sean followed her gesture to a small side table sitting next to the couch. "You had a computer there?"

"Yes. It was practically brand new."

"You're sure you didn't leave it somewhere else in the house?"

49

She stared at him with wide eyes. "I don't think so. I wouldn't leave it in the car, so upstairs would be the only other place it could be, but I'm sure I left it down here."

Sean would need information on the laptop, but that could wait. First... "Okay, we need to look upstairs, which means crossing the hallway area."

He met Felicity Pope's gaze. Her top lip trembled.

"Mrs. Pope, try not to focus on the blood but head directly to the second floor, okay?"

Her head bobbed up and down with a quick jerk.

Sean moved over to the hallway. "I'll lead the way, and you step where I do, understand?"

He didn't wait for an answer but made his first step to a small spot of open floor, then another to the base of the staircase, and then finally, pushed himself onto the bottom landing. Moving up three more steps, he turned and watched as Felicity, her eyes fixed on the stairs, followed the same path, and lastly, Monique.

When they were all on the landing, Sean headed quickly up the stairs, drawing the women away from the foyer. At the top, he let the women pass him so they could resume the search.

Almost robotic in nature now, Felicity moved from one room to the next. In the spare bedroom that held a suitcase, Monique scanned the dresser and side table. "My laptop isn't up here. Like I said, I'm sure it was downstairs in the living room."

Sean nodded. "Okay. Nothing else of yours is missing?"

Monique picked through the suitcase then shook her head. "Looks like everything else is here."

They moved on to the bathroom then the master bedroom. Felicity took longer here, mostly sorting through her jewelry, going over it twice to make sure she wasn't missing anything.

Finally, she looked up. "I think it's all here."

"Good." Sean recalled his promise to let them get a few things. "Each of you can gather some clothes, but I need to photograph them before we leave."

Both women nodded and set about gathering a few items. It didn't take long, and after logging everything, Sean headed for the top of the stairs. This time, while descending, there would be no avoiding the sight at the bottom.

Sean led the way down, repeating the step over into the living room, then waited for the ladies to make their way past him and into the kitchen before he followed.

Monique had found a small overnight bag in her mother's closet and put everything in it. Mrs. Pope didn't have to carry anything—which was good—because just getting down the stairs and out the door appeared to be all the poor woman could manage by then.

Nobody uttered a word.

At the kitchen door, Sean paused. "Anything else you can think of?"

She shook her head. "I don't think so."

He opened the back door. "Okay. Let's step outside."

They returned to the sunshine, leaving the sights and smells of the home behind.

Sean studied Felicity's face, her eyes rimmed red. "Are you okay?"

She nodded weakly.

"You did great."

A shrug.

While Sean had been waiting for the ladies to gather a few things, he'd considered the missing items. The computer would be easy to resell for cash, and if the intruder had taken it from the living room, he did so before attacking Rodney Pope—even the luminol search hadn't found bloody footsteps in there.

That would suggest Mr. Pope interrupted the burglary early on, if that was indeed the motive for the crime.

The same held true for the cash. Still, the casino cup was troublesome. Nothing had been turned over or strewn around indicating someone had been in there looking for stuff to steal.

Maybe Rodney Pope retrieved the money in an effort to pacify his attackers?

That scenario didn't fit with the idea he was attacked as he came through the door, but anything was still possible at this point.

Was the money in plain view, or did the name on the cup attract the killer's attention?

Did they just get lucky and find the cash?

"Mrs. Pope, could you see the money in the cup?"

"What do you mean?"

"Was it in view? Or did someone need to know where it was?"

She cocked her head to one side. "I suppose you could see the money through the plastic—I'm not sure."

"Is the cup from the Harrah's in North Carolina?"

"Yes."

The closest gambling spot to Metro Atlanta, *Harrah's Cherokee Valley River* was just over two hours away. Lots of folks from the city went up there on their leisure time.

"You said the money was from your last trip. When was that?"

"Last Wednesday."

"Was your husband with you?"

"No. He doesn't...didn't go anymore. A friend and I would ride up with on one of those excursion buses."

"This friend—who is it?"

"Andre Gordon."

Sean got out his notepad. "How long have you and Mr. Gordon known each other?"

"About three years. My husband and I met Andre on one of those bus trips. When Rodney stopped going with me, Andre and I continued riding up together."

Alarm bells went off in Sean's head. "So, Mr. Gordon was with you last Wednesday?"

"Yes."

"Does Mr. Gordon know where you keep your gambling money?"

Felicity stared at him, her eyes glazing over as if she weighed the insinuation packed within Sean's question. "I suppose I mentioned it...but Andre would never do something like this."

"I understand, but I'll still need his contact information."

She reached into her pocket and extracted her cellphone then read off the number.

Sean wrote it down. "Mrs. Pope, did your husband know about you sharing these trips with Andre Gordon?"

"Of course."

"And he didn't have a problem with it?"

She shook her head. "Rodney didn't care."

Sean glanced at Monique. She was watching him intently. He sensed his next question would not be well received.

"I know it's a difficult time, but I'm afraid I have to ask…"

Monique moved closer. Her stare seemed to carry a warning for him to be careful. He ignored it.

"Mrs. Pope, was your relationship with Andre Gordon of a romantic nature?"

Monique scowled. "Detective, is that really…?"

Pope cut her daughter off. "No! Definitely not!"

Sean pretended not to see Monique Butler's glare. "I'm sorry, but I had to ask. Thank you for your honesty."

He had probably pushed them as far as they could go for now. He glanced at his watch. The tour had taken longer than he'd hoped—he would be late to Janine Evans's place.

"Miss Butler, you have my card, correct?"

"Yes."

"Please email me any information about your laptop that you have. Brand, serial number, even a photo if you have one."

"Okay, I can do that."

"Good."

Sean turned toward the driveway, and the women followed. He escorted them out to their car, watched them drive off, then went to his own vehicle down the street. Returning to the house, he re-entered and bagged the plastic cup. After his meeting with Janine Evans, he would get it over to forensics.

Home of Janine Evans
Myrtle Street NE
Midtown Atlanta
12:45 p.m.

Sean had been fortunate with the traffic and was only running fifteen minutes late when he pulled up at the home of Janine Evans. After parking on the street, he took the steps up to the house two at a time then rang the bell.

Moments later, a voice came from behind the door. "Who is it?"

Sean held up his badge in front of the peephole. "Detective Sparks—Atlanta Police Department."

A latch flipped, and the door opened. "Hi."

"Miss Janine Evans?"

"Actually, it's Mrs. Evans."

"May I come in?"

The woman pulled the door wide. "Of course."

Sean stepped inside and put away his badge. "I'm sorry I'm late."

Mrs. Evans closed the door and turned to face him. "It's no problem."

"Is there somewhere we can sit and talk?"

She gestured at the living room on their left. "Sure. In here."

Sean followed her and sat in the loveseat she pointed at.

Janine Evans pulled a pink bathrobe tight around her and crossed her arms over her chest as she lowered herself into a chair opposite him. Her brown hair was cut just above

55

collar length and clung to her neck, obviously still wet from a shower. Her round face and smooth skin were highlighted by full lips, but her bright-green eyes caught and held his attention. Even though they were dulled by pain, it was clear she had inherited them from her father.

"I'm very sorry for your loss."

"Thank you." She studied him, chewing her bottom lip with apprehension.

"Is Mr. Evans home?"

"We're in the process of getting a divorce. He lives in Alaska."

"I see." He took out his notepad. "When was the last time you saw your father?"

Her eyes reddened. "Last Wednesday. We had lunch."

The same day Mrs. Pope went on her gambling junket.

Sean tested Mrs. Evans. "Was your mother-in-law with you?"

Her face curled into a look of contempt. "I haven't spoken to that woman in nearly three years."

Sean hoped he'd concealed his surprise. "You don't get along?"

"Oh, we did in the beginning."

"The beginning?"

"When she and Dad first got married."

"Not so lately?"

She shifted uncomfortably. "Dad and Felicity turned out to be like oil and water. He's…was…kind, mellow, and considerate. She's controlling, churlish, and vindictive. Either she hid it well when they were dating, or Dad ignored the warning signs. Either way, despite him trying to make it work for a long time, it fell apart about eighteen months ago."

56

Sean was writing as fast as he could. This was news to him and would all need to be verified, but it certainly cast Felicity Pope in a different light.

Perhaps that was intentional.

"What specifically happened?"

"My father finally decided it was hopeless. He wasn't happy, so he moved into a separate bedroom and told Felicity he wanted a divorce."

Sean looked up. "He didn't move out?"

"Dad had money tied up in the house. He'd put a roof on the place, new windows and flooring throughout, and new kitchen appliances. His lawyer advised him that if he left, it might look to the court as if he had abandoned the marriage *and* its assets."

While this might sound counter-intuitive to most, Sean had run into the same logic on a previous case. A man had stayed in his home, living in the basement and avoiding his wife, so the court wouldn't think he had ceded his parental interests in their child. They ended up in a physical altercation, and he beat her up, ending any question of who got custody.

"Detective?"

"Yes?"

"Is my mother-in-law a suspect?"

"At this point, I haven't cleared anyone, but she does have an alibi. Do you think she could have hurt your father?"

"Not only do *I* think she could hurt him, but my Dad was sure she *would*—given the chance. When we had lunch last week, he described taking a chair and placing it under his bedroom doorknob when he slept. He was afraid of her."

This picture did not mesh with the frail woman Sean had just escorted through the scene of her husband's murder. "Did he mention anything specific—like a threat?"

"Yes! She said many times she was going to end him for what he had done to her!"

Sean raised an eyebrow. "End him? She used those words?"

"That's what he told me. I wanted him to get out, forget about the money, but he was stubborn. If she didn't do it herself, then she had to be in on it."

"Mrs. Evans, I promise you that we'll look at everyone, your mother-in-law included, very carefully."

"My dad didn't deserve to die like that. If you want to know more about his character, you should speak to Natalie."

"Natalie?"

"Natalie Dennis. She was my father's second wife. She's remarried now, but they spent six years together."

"Do you know how I can reach her?"

"No, but I believe she lives in Marietta."

She sank back into her chair and blew out a breath. The effort of revealing all this seemed suddenly to take its toll on the woman, but Sean still had a couple more questions.

"Can you think of anyone else who might want to hurt your dad?"

"No. Like I said, Dad was a mellow soul."

"What about Monique Butler?"

She shrugged. "I only met her a few times. Dad said she took after her mother, but I never saw anything mean from her."

Sean closed his notepad and pulled out a business card. "Thank you for speaking with me. Please call if you think of anything else."

She nodded but didn't reach for the card. He laid it on the table and stood. "I'll see myself out."

Her eyes brimmed over with tears that ran unchecked down her cheeks and onto her robe.

"Detective?"

"Ma'am?"

She pulled a pink sleeve across her eyes. "Find out who did this to my Dad—please. He was all the family I had left."

Sean swallowed hard. "I'll do everything in my power—I promise."

She nodded and buried her face in her hands. He wanted to say something, do something to help, but didn't know what. Instead, he quietly made his way outside.

Sean stood on the small porch and looked out at the homes on the block, most of which had some sort of Christmas decorations on them. The holiday scene amplified the pain of the woman inside the house he'd just left. Was there ever a good moment to lose a loved one? No…he couldn't think of one, but Christmas seemed the worst time of all. The holiday cheer of others only served to magnify the sense of loss.

Sean regularly struggled with a sort of guilt when he did notifications. Tasked with delivering the most painful news a family can get, he had to do his best to stay detached, which concealed the empathy he was feeling for them. The holidays just made things ten times worse.

He looked at his watch. The autopsy was scheduled for 3:30 p.m., two hours away. Time enough to drop off the plastic cup first. He also wanted to schedule another chat with Felicity Pope, this time without her daughter present.

Suddenly overcome with weariness, he forced himself forward and down the steps.

Georgia Bureau of Investigation Headquarters
Panthersville Road
Southeast of Atlanta
2:30 p.m.

Located on the outside edge of the perimeter loop, the Georgia Bureau of Investigation building sat just fifteen minutes from downtown. The brown brick building with white curved awnings rambled across several acres, some of the structure consisting of three floors while other sections had just two. Evidence processing for all the area law enforcement agencies was conducted here.

Sean had high hopes for the item he wanted tested, and even if they didn't find a good print, maybe they'd be able to extract some sweat DNA.

Nothing made up for good-old hard work when it came to solving cases—something Lance Henderson had never tired of telling Sean—but the fact was, DNA was a game changer. Sean was like every other detective; if they got a DNA hit, they felt like a prospector who'd found gold flakes in his river pan. High fives all around.

Sean presented his ID, checked his gun, then headed for the forensic lab. Sterile, bright, and busy were the three terms that best described this part of the facility. Tasha King was the lead tech on duty and approached him as soon as he came through the lab door.

"Hey, Sean. How are you?"

"Good, Tasha. You?"

"Great." Born to Japanese parents, she always wore her waist-length, straight jet-black hair tied in a long ponytail. She had a quick wit and a gentle smile that came easily, even when dealing with the more gruesome aspects of her job. "Bring me something to play with?"

He held out the baggie. "As a matter of fact, yes."

She took it with two gloved hands, staring at the cup as if it were the crown jewels. "Is this from the Pope homicide? I heard you were lead on that one."

"It is, and you heard right."

"Okay. I should be able to get something done on this before the end of the day."

"Perfect. You know how to reach me."

"Yes, sir."

He smiled. "I'll be waiting with baited breath!"

She laughed. "Unfortunately, I don't have any results for you yet on the other evidence we gathered."

"I guess it won't do any good to stamp my feet and look annoyed?"

She shook her head. "You can if you want, but it doesn't work for anyone else."

With a smirk, she went back toward her work station.

Sean retraced his steps out of the building, got back into his car, and headed for the autopsy. As he pulled out of the parking lot, his phone rang. When he glanced at the number, a smile crossed his face.

"Hi, beautiful."

"Flattery will get you everywhere, mister."

He could picture Mariah's warm smile. "That's what I'm counting on."

"How's it going?"

"The question should be, where's it going?"

"Okay. Where's it going?"

He sighed. "Nowhere right now." His Christmas gift for her crossed his mind.

Will I be able to deliver it before the holiday has passed? He could only hope so.

"Having a tough time with your case?"

"Yeah, so far anyway. Nothing solid to go on. How was your day?"

"Okay. Christmas break begins after school tomorrow, and we have our class party in the morning, so the kiddos are pretty hyped up." Mariah taught special needs kids at Beecher Hill Elementary School on the west side of the city. "Are you going to get away for dinner?"

"Hard to know. I'm on my way to the autopsy now."

"Ewww, I don't know how you can go to those."

He laughed. "Well, we're even, because I don't know how you have the patience for your job."

"Fair enough, I guess. Call me if you can get away?"

"I will. Love you."

"Love you more."

He grinned. "Not possible."

Fulton County Medical Examiner's Office
430 Pryor Street SW
Mechanicsville Neighborhood
West of Downtown
3:20 p.m.

Sitting in the shadows of the tall, downtown structures, the coroner's office was much like the GBI building Sean had just come from—an ordinary brown brick structure meant to allow the people who worked there to do their jobs without attracting undue attention.

He parked and made his way through the sinking afternoon sunlight toward the entrance. After checking in, he went down a long hallway toward the autopsy theaters. He stopped outside number 6 and peered through the window.

Ryan Carter waved Sean inside. "Don't stand out there. Come on in for a better view."

Sean smiled and pushed through the doors into the chilly room and joined the doc at the side of the stainless-steel table supporting Rodney Pope's body. The gurney had been pushed up against a large, three-bay sink, making for easier clean up after the procedure. One end of the table was formed into the shape of a funnel and hung over the sink bays.

Rodney Pope's sternum was open, and his organs had already been removed.

"I got an early start," Ryan said.

Sean gave him a crooked smirk. "I can see that."

Doc pointed at the heart, still in the hanging scale, which was not unlike the one used to weigh fruit at the grocery store. "I figured you'd seen all this stuff before. The real interesting part is going to be around the head."

"Then I can assume you haven't found any other injuries on the body?"

"Yes, you can assume that, and you'd be correct. No gunshot wounds, stab wounds, or even blunt force trauma to places you might expect, such as his forearms or hands. It's as if he never defended himself."

Sean stared at Pope's head, which had taken a horrendous beating. "You think he was out from the first blow?"

Carter nodded. "That's what everything is telling me so far."

He removed the heart from the scale and bagged it for dissection later. An assistant laid it with the other organs sitting on a rolling cart then rolled it out of the way.

Carter pulled a lighted magnifier into position just inches from the dead man's face. "Now for the skull."

He stared at the injury on the forehead, then moving the magnifier, he examined one eyebrow at a time. Each individual blow had to be photographed, studied, measured, and marked on a drawing. It was tedious, time consuming work. All the while, Carter talked into a microphone suspended above the gurney.

"Face and forehead show signs of perimortem bruising. Wounds appear to be similar and are classified as lacerations with avulsion at several points."

Sean had heard most of these terms before. *Perimortem* meant the bruising occurred at or near the time of death.

64

Lacerations referred to a splitting or tearing of the skin over the wound. *Avulsion* was a new one for him, but he'd wait until Carter was done to ask.

Carter took a scalpel and cut loose what skin was still attached, peeling the layer back to expose the cranium. He pulled the magnifier in for a close look at the damage to the front of the skull and restarted the process of measuring.

The description continued as well. "Damage to the skull is primarily a depressed fracture, and there is evidence of intracranial bleeds, specifically epidural and subdural. Examination of brain required to confirm intracerebral bleeding. Object used to make injuries was rounded, smooth, and may have linear aspects as well."

The medical examiner reached up and shut off the mic. "I imagine you have things to do, so I'll summarize."

Sean pulled out his notepad. "Please do."

"Mr. Pope would have died quickly, possibly from the initial blow. He was hit with such force that fragments of bone were driven into his brain. The weapon will likely be something along the lines of a length of pipe, baseball bat, or a similar smooth, elongated object."

"Got it." Sean jotted down the information. "By the way, what's an avulsion?"

"It's a laceration where the skin is torn free from the surrounding flesh and its supporting structures underneath."

Sean stared at Carter. The medical examiner grinned.

"Suffice it to say that whoever hit this guy meant to kill him. The force required to make these kinds of injuries is extreme."

Sean tucked away his pad. "Copy that. Send me the report in the morning?"

"You got it."

"Thanks, Doc."

Sean made his way out of the cold room, rubbing his hands together to restore some feeling to the end of his fingers. He checked the time—5:45.

He didn't have anything else that needed done immediately. Or maybe, he just didn't have the energy to tackle something new—he had been awake some thirty hours. He headed out to the car and called Mariah.

"Hello?"

"Hey, it's me. I'm calling it a day. Want to grab a bite before I crash?"

"Sure. What did you have in mind?"

"Pizza."

"Didn't you just leave an autopsy?"

"Yeah."

She grunted. "You detective types. Cut your finger and you need help with a bandage. Go to a gruesome procedure and it makes you hungry."

"What's your point?"

"Where did you want to meet?"

"My place?"

"Okay."

Exhaustion washed over him. "And Mariah?"

"Yes?"

"Could you pick up the pizza? I'm beat."

"Some date!" Her voice softened. "Of course. See you soon."

"You're the best."

Tuesday, December 19

Home of Detective Sean Sparks
Camden Vantage Apartments
Sweet Auburn Neighborhood
East of Downtown Atlanta
8:15 a.m.

Sean and Mariah had polished off the pizza with gusto, but almost immediately afterward, he'd nodded off. She'd set his alarm for him before leaving, which was awesome, but she'd set it for an hour later than he'd have preferred. After climbing out of the shower, he was throwing on clothes when his phone rang.

With one sock on, and while tugging at the other one, he cradled the phone on his shoulder.

"Hello?"

"Detective Sparks?"

"Yes."

"This is…"

The phone slid off his shoulder. "Oh, man…" He gave up on the sock and snatched the phone off the floor. "I'm sorry. Who is this?"

"Tasha King. Are you okay?"

Sean grimaced. "Yeah, just sock trouble."

"Okay…no need to explain. I have the initial report on your crime scene."

"Excellent."

"You want me to go over it now?"

"Normally, I'd say yes, but I'm running late. Can you send it over to the precinct?"

"Of course—no problem. Let me know if you have any questions."

"Great...oh, Tasha?"

"Yeah?"

"I did have one. The plastic cup—you get anything off it?"

"Yes, a couple prints."

Sean's hopes soared. "Did you run them yet?"

"I did. One matched the prints taken from Felicity Pope at the time of her initial interview. The other one, which I believe to be a thumb, did not come back with a hit on AFIS."

"Those the only ones?"

"On the mug, yes."

"Okay, thanks. I'll read the rest when I get to the station."

"No problem."

"Bye." He threw the phone onto the bed and finished putting on his sock. With just one unidentified print on the plastic cup, which could belong to anyone from the casino or elsewhere, it was a setback for his investigation—and a crappy start to his day.

He grabbed a jacket and jogged out to his car.

Atlanta Police Headquarters
Homicide Division
226 Peachtree Street SW
Downtown Atlanta
9:35 a.m.

Sean was on his second cup of coffee and just finishing his review of the forensic report when he got an idea. Picking up the phone, he called the Fulton County 911 dispatch. Within minutes, he had a copy of the emergency call made by Monique Butler on its way to him.

When he opened his email folder, he found it and another message, this one from Monique Butler. He clicked on Monique's first.

Detective Sparks,
My laptop was a Microsoft Surface 3. I don't have serial numbers or such yet. Those will have to wait until I get back to Savannah and look through my papers.

Sincerely,
Monique Butler

Out of curiosity, Sean did a search for the computer name given by Monique. The Surface 3 retailed for roughly thirteen hundred dollars.

No wonder they took it.

He would get the information on the computer put out to pawn shops, but without a serial number, it would be a shot in the dark.

Next, he wanted to hear the 911 call. After opening the secure email from the dispatch center, he clicked on the icon to download the audio file. He put on a set of earbuds and played the call back.

"Fulton County 9-1-1. What is your emergency?"

"My stepfather is down in our front hallway. I think he's been attacked."

"What is the address?"

"2905 Renfro Drive."

"What is your stepfather's name?"

"Rodney Pope."

"And what is your name?"

"Monique Butler."

"Okay. Stay with me. I have emergency personnel on the way. Is Mr. Pope conscious?"

"I don't think so. I don't know."

"Are you able to check for a pulse?"

"No. He's lying against the door."

"What about his chest? Can you see if it's rising and falling?"

"No! I don't know."

"Very well. Are you in a safe place?"

"Yes, at least, I think so. I'm in my car with my mother."

"Good. Stay put until the officer approaches you, understand?"

"Yes."

He played it back again—listening closely to each word. The level of panic seemed appropriate, as did the fear in her voice.

He listened a third time. Something bothered him, but what? The fourth time through, he heard it.

"My stepfather is down in our front hallway. I think he's been attacked."

She'd used the word attacked.

Would she have reason to believe he'd been attacked? Would that be a safe assumption based on her glimpse through a door sitting ajar?

He ran a hand across his chin, the course stubble reminding him he'd forgotten to shave. He'd be rough-looking by the end of the day.

He played the recording once more. Nothing else stood out. He took out the earphone, looked up the number for Officer Tom Bradley, and dialed.

"Hello?"

"Officer Bradley?"

"Yes."

"This is Detective Sparks."

"Oh, hi, Detective. What can I do for you?"

"Just a quick question. Did you peer through the front door at the body before going to the back door?"

"Yes."

"Could you see Mr. Pope's head?"

A long pause followed. "I'm not sure. I remember seeing the legs and feet, then choosing not to force my way in. I can't say for sure if I saw his head or not."

"Okay. Thanks for your time."

"Is that it?"

71

"For right now."

"Okay. Any progress finding the killer?"

"Not yet."

"Good luck."

"Thanks." Sean hung up. It was time for another sit down with the two women in this case. He wanted to talk to Felicity Pope first and dialed her number.

"Hello?"

"Mrs. Pope?"

"No, this is Monique—her daughter."

"Miss Butler. This is Detective Sparks."

"Yes, Detective. Any news?"

"No, I'm afraid not, but thank you for your email."

"Of course. Is there anything else we can do?"

Funny you should ask. "Actually, I need to speak with your mother further. Could she come down to the station this afternoon?"

"I don't see why not. What time?"

Shouldn't she ask her mother? "One o'clock?"

"Very well. We'll see you then."

"Goodbye." Sean hung up.

"Detective Sparks?"

He turned to see the Lieutenant leaning out of her office door. "Hey, Lieutenant"

"A moment of your time?"

"Yes, ma'am."

She retreated to her office. He stood, gathered the forensic report, then followed her.

"Close the door, Sean."

He did, then sat in the chair across from her.

The office was not large; in fact, it was pretty cramped. Still, the lieutenant had made it her own with a bookcase wedged into the corner and photos and commendations covering the walls behind her. A door with distorted glass on the top half, like Sean remembered from elementary school, provided a bit of privacy.

Nevertheless, when things got heated, which they sometimes did, everyone in the squad room could hear it. For some, this would be a problem, but not for Lieutenant Shannon Mitchell—she wasn't shy about her opinions, and she was usually right.

She leaned back in her chair and met his gaze. "Fill me in."

"Well…" He opened the forensic report. "The evidence processing wasn't much help. One unknown fingerprint was found but without a hit, and the shoe impression in the back alley turned out to match one of the victim's boots. Several bloody footsteps were photographed inside the house, but they were too badly smudged for the techs to identify the shoe make or model."

Mitchell steepled her fingers in front of her. "That's disappointing."

"Indeed, though they were able to approximate the size—between eight and nine."

"That narrows it down to about half the city's population."

He grimaced. "Yeah, I know."

She supported her chin with her fingers. "Motive?"

He set the report down and crossed his arms in front of his chest. "Some items were stolen, and since it appears likely

73

that the victim was attacked the moment he got into the house, it's possible he interrupted a burglary."

"What's your gut telling you?"

He shrugged. "I'm not sure. The autopsy revealed severe damage to Mr. Pope's head, which led Doc Carter to the conclusion that the attacker was intent on killing Pope. That suggests a personal attack driven by emotion."

"What about the weapon?"

"Carter couldn't say for sure, but he thinks something long and cylindrical is likely."

Mitchell closed her eyes. He waited.

"Your search of the back yards—any luck?"

He shook his head. "A witness did give us enough to suggest the killer or killers escaped through the alley that runs behind the house."

She nodded. "So, now the big one. Any suspects?"

He sighed. "No one solid. There's Mrs. Pope and her daughter, but they were together and appear to have a good alibi. I haven't corroborated it yet. There's a person of interest—Andre Gordon—who's an acquaintance of Mrs. Pope. I haven't had a chance to meet with him, though."

Mitchell sat forward. "Sounds like you have a full day ahead. Henderson is still tied up, so keep after it. I'll cut him loose if I can, but I wouldn't hold your breath."

"Yes, ma'am."

"Anything else I should know?"

"Just this. I interviewed Rodney Pope's daughter from his first marriage. She claims her father was afraid of his wife and was sleeping with his bedroom door blockaded."

Mitchell raised an eyebrow. "Really? Did the daughter say why Mr. Pope was afraid?"

74

"She did. He and Felicity Pope were going through an acrimonious divorce."

"The spouse is always a suspect until cleared."

Sean shrugged. "Yes, but I'm not sure it fits. Especially considering her alibi, but I'm planning on talking with her again. Also, she and Miss Butler were checked for blood that night but came up clean."

"I never said this job was easy, Sean."

"No, ma'am."

"Unless you need something before then, get with me again tomorrow."

"Copy that."

He picked up his report and returned to his desk. Hashing out the facts with his boss served to cast a darker pall over his day. He needed a break, something to latch onto and run with.

He found the number for Andre Gordon and dialed it. It rang several times before a man picked up.

"Hello?"

"Andre Gordon, please."

"Speaking."

"Mr. Gordon, my name is Detective Sparks with Atlanta PD."

"Ah, yes. Felicity mentioned you might call."

To Sean, a red flag waved when witnesses communicated.

Did Mrs. Pope give him a heads up on what to say?

Still, he hadn't told Felicity Pope *not* to call her friend, so that was on him.

"I'm investigating the death of Rodney Pope and was hoping to speak with you. Is there a time we could meet?"

"I'm free this morning."

"Great. I can come to you."

"Very well. 371 Augusta Ave."

Sean jotted it down. "I'll head over now."

"See you soon."

Sean hung up and headed out to his car. He punched the address into his GPS and found Mr. Gordon lived in Grant Park, just a few minutes away. A check of his watch told him he would be back in plenty of time to meet Felicity Pope.

Home of Andre Gordon
371 Augusta Avenue SE
Grant Park Neighborhood
11:00 a.m.

Just southeast of downtown, Grant Park was filled with Victorian mansions and Craftsman-style bungalows. Best known for being home to Zoo Atlanta with its popular panda and tiger exhibits, the area was popular with young locals who enjoyed Tex-Mex and pub fare.

Andre Gordon's tiny home was a Craftsman sided in light blue, but it reminded Sean more of the shotgun homes of Mississippi and Louisiana. Still, it was neat and inviting. He parked on the street and went up toward the front door, which opened just as he stepped onto the porch.

"Detective Sparks, please come in."

"Thank you, sir."

Sean entered the small foyer, and like his first impression suggested, he could see all the way through the home to the back door.

Gordon shut the door. "Would you like some coffee?"

"That would be nice."

"Good. Follow me."

They walked back to the kitchen, and Sean took the seat Gordon offered. The silver-haired, dark-skinned gentleman talked as he poured.

"It's a terrible thing, what happened to poor Rodney. He was a nice man."

"I understand you met him on a gambling junket."

"That's correct." He handed a steaming mug to Sean. "I'm guessing you take your coffee black. Am I right?"

Sean smiled. "You are."

Gordon beamed. "I like trying to judge people's coffee choice."

"Well, you're one for one with me."

"I wish I could say that was my average, but I'm closer to fifty percent." He laughed. "Anyway, what can I help you with?"

Sean noticed a plastic cup bearing the Harrah's Casino logo. It was identical to the one from the Pope residence. He gestured toward it with his mug. "Mrs. Pope had a casino cup like that."

Gordon answered without turning to look at it. "We got them at the same time. Some sort of a promotion."

Sean set down his mug and pulled out his notepad. "Could you tell me about Rodney Pope?"

"As I said, he was a nice man. I only visited with him maybe three or four times before he stopped going on the gambling excursions."

"Did you ever meet with him aside from those?"

"No. Just never had cause to."

"How would you describe your relationship with Mrs. Pope?"

He shrugged. "Friendly. We had a good time at the casino."

"Was there any romantic feelings between you?"

Gordon's mood seemed to change. His smile evaporated like a ghost in the sunlight. "Depends on who you ask. If I have my way, she and I might have a future."

Sean's interest spiked. "She didn't feel the same way?"

"I don't think so. She was so focused on the situation with Rodney that she refused to entertain the idea. At least, that was my impression."

"Did you ever hear Mrs. Pope speak of hurting her husband?"

"Felicity? Nah, I don't think she had it in her, though she has a temper, that's for sure."

"What makes you say that?"

"She once thought a dealer had cheated her. She came unglued. The casino gave her the money back just to appease her."

"Had the dealer cheated?"

"I doubt it. But that didn't dissuade Felicity."

"Mr. Gordon, where were you Sunday night?"

"Here."

"All night?"

"All night. Didn't do anything but watch some TV."

78

"Is there anyone who can verify that?"

Gordon waved a hand around him. "Nobody here but these walls, but, Detective, I wouldn't hurt Rodney or anyone else."

Sean put away his notepad and stood. He caught a glimpse of Gordon's boots. "Do you mind me asking what size shoe you wear?"

Gordon seemed surprised and glanced down at his feet. "Uh…eight and a half. Why?"

Sean smiled. "It's a detective thing—sort of like guessing how someone takes their coffee."

Gordon smiled. "I see."

"Thank you for your time, sir. I'll let myself out."

Back at his car, Sean considered the interview.

Size eight and a half is smack in the middle of the shoe-size range. Add to that unrequited love and no alibi, he makes for a great suspect.

Mr. Gordon bore further examination.

Sean's stomach had already informed him it was nearly lunchtime, but he checked his watch anyway. With over an hour before Felicity Pope and Monique Butler showed up, he considered his options. A Chick-Fil-A was nearby, and a chicken sandwich sounded really good.

ATLANTA HOMICIDE

Interview Room 2
Atlanta Police Headquarters
Homicide Division
226 Peachtree Street SW
Downtown Atlanta
1:05 p.m.

Sean returned from Andre Gordon's to find Monique Butler pacing in the front lobby of the precinct. He went over to say hello.

"Thanks for coming—"

Butler lunged in his direction. "What is the meaning of having my mother taken back without me?"

"Meaning? I'm afraid I don't understand."

"My mother is very frail right now. She needs my support."

"It's simply protocol, Miss Butler. In a homicide case, an interview with the spouse is always conducted one on one."

"Without a lawyer?"

Sean kept his demeanor flat, despite finding the reaction interesting, even troubling.

"It's an *interview*, Miss Butler. She is not being interrogated, and she is not under arrest. If she wants to have an attorney present, she certainly can. Did she make that request?"

"Well…no." She glanced around the lobby, perhaps suddenly aware of the scene she was creating. "I'm just worried about her."

"I completely understand. How about this? I'm going to speak with her now, so I'll make sure she understands that it's only an interview and she can leave at any time if she feels like it."

With nothing to sustain the outburst, she dropped her voice to nearly a whisper. "I would appreciate it."

The daughter's concern was warranted but the reaction excessive—a red flag in Sean's book. He forced a smile. "You have my word. Please make yourself comfortable, and I'll keep the discussion as brief as possible."

He didn't wait for her approval. He strode to the security door and was buzzed through, leaving Butler standing in the middle of the lobby.

He stopped at his desk to pick up a digital recorder. He preferred to have a personal copy of his interviews, even though all interview rooms had both video and audio recording.

Tapping twice on the door, he entered and nodded to Felicity Pope. "Good afternoon, Mrs. Pope."

She managed a half-hearted smile, and while she looked far from refreshed, it did appear she had gathered her wits about her. "Hello, Detective Sparks."

"Would you like something to drink?"

"No, thank you."

Sean pulled out the chair opposite her and laid the recorder on the table. "I'd like to record our talk, if that's okay."

She nodded, and he clicked the machine to start.

"Before we begin, I promised your daughter I would make something clear to you."

ATLANTA HOMICIDE

Mrs. Pope, clutching the same coat she'd worn the first time he met her, but in a grey sweater and black slacks this time, fluffed the scarf around her neck and rolled her eyes.

"Oh, Monique. I hope she didn't create a fuss. She's very protective of me."

"No, it was fine. She just wanted me to make sure you understand this is just an interview, and you can leave if you feel the need to."

She pushed a wisp of gray hair out of her eyes and met his gaze. "I'll be fine."

"Good." He opened his notebook. "The purpose for our talk today is to go over some of the personal details in your marriage to Mr. Pope. It's not done to pry but because some things are important to cover in any investigation. I'm sure you can understand."

She nodded and folded her hands in her lap, clutching tighter to the coat.

"How would you describe your marriage to Mr. Pope?"

She shifted uncomfortably. "Great, at first. He was kind, attentive, and loving."

"And lately?"

Her lips curled into a snarl. "Lately, I discovered what kind of man he really was."

"What do you mean by that?"

"Rodney turned on me. He was a selfish man."

"Janine Evans informed me that you and Mr. Pope were in the process of getting a divorce. Is that correct?"

"Yes."

"But Mr. Pope remained in the house. That must have been awkward."

82

"You could say that, but he kept to himself, and I did the same."

"I understand money was the main contention."

Her face reddened. "It was always that way with him. He didn't love me—he just wanted my money!"

Sean made a note, pausing long enough to make the woman shift uncomfortably.

"My understanding was that Mr. Pope had a pension and some savings."

"Sure, but I paid for the gambling junkets and all the bills."

"Was Mr. Pope a heavy gambler?"

"Not really."

"So, the money for the gambling junkets was yours?"

"Yes."

"But most of the money was spent by him?"

"No...not most."

Sean sat back and regarded the woman. Her chest heaved slightly.

"Was money an issue from day one, or did it change at some point?"

"Look, the daily bills and such were not the main problem. It was his desire to take half the money from the sale of the house that was ludicrous. I bought that house!"

"That made you angry, I can see."

"Wouldn't you be?"

Sean ignored the question. "But according to Mrs. Evans, your husband put a considerable amount of money into the home by paying for things such as a roof and appliances."

"Oh, please." Her tone reeked with disdain. "A few minor repairs was all. It was about the money from the beginning. He was a con man who thought he could take me for a bundle, but I showed him."

Sean sat forward and locked eyes with her. "Showed him how?"

Her eyes widened. "I didn't kill him! That's not what I meant."

"What did you mean?"

"I refused to be bullied. I countersued for divorce and to keep my money."

"How did Mr. Pope take that?"

She rotated in her seat, turning herself sideways to Sean and creating a buffer zone. "I don't know. Not well, I suppose, but we weren't talking. You should ask his girlfriend."

"I'm sorry?" Despite himself, Sean let his eyebrows spike. "His girlfriend?"

She scoffed. "You're some detective. You haven't learned about little miss husband stealer?"

"I guess not."

"Where do you think he was going every night on his walks?"

Sean pulled his pad toward him. "Do you know who this woman is?"

"Sure. I got suspicious and followed him one night. He thought he was smart—what a joke. He left his car at Scott Park then walked to her house."

"Do you know this woman's name?"

"Sally Robinson. She lives over on Collier Drive."

"How long did you suspect this was going on?"

"A year, eighteen months maybe. He didn't deny it when I confronted him. He had probably picked her as his next victim."

"To steal from—is what you're suggesting?"

"You bet. You should ask his second wife, too. I'm sure he took her to the cleaners, as well."

Sean already planned to contact Natalie Dennis. "Since we last spoke, have you thought of anyone who might have wanted to hurt Mr. Pope?"

"No, but..." She opened her purse and reached in. "Monique said to give you this."

She held out a slip of paper.

Sean took it. "What is it?"

"It's the receipt from our dinner at the Colonnade. My daughter thought you might want it."

"Actually, yes. Thank you."

She snapped her purse shut. "I'm tired, Detective Sparks. Are we done?"

"Yes, ma'am. Thank you for your time."

She stood. "When will we be able to get back into the house?"

"Soon, I hope." Sean shut off his recorder. "I'll walk you out."

As he led her back out, she followed close on his heels and bolted when she saw her daughter.

Sean stood by the security door, watching the animated exchange between the two women as they left. It looked to Sean as if Monique was giving her mother the third degree.

Man, would I love to be privy to that conversation.

ATLANTA HOMICIDE

The Colonnade Restaurant
1879 Cheshire Bridge Road NE
Lenox Park
Northeast of Downtown
3:45 p.m.

The Colonnade Restaurant had been an Atlanta staple since it opened in 1927. Originally started in a white-columned, antebellum-style home, it had been moved to its current location in 1962. Huge portions of chicken, pork, or seafood were followed by homemade dressings, sauces, pies, and yeast rolls. The Colonnade reflected a time in the South when home-cooked meals were shared on bountiful tables by grateful families.

Sean had eaten there several times and knew the route from the station almost as well as his way home. It took him just over thirty minutes to pull up to the low-slung white building with windows all across the front. Inside, the lull between lunch and the dinner rush meant the manager, Willie Fleming, had time to speak with him.

"Detective Sparks, nice to see you again."

Willie's smile was perpetually on display. Whether the restaurant was packed or empty, he seemed happy to be at work. "Here for a late bite?"

"Afraid not, Willie. My visit is for official business today."

"Oh? Have we run afoul of Atlanta's finest?"

Sean smiled. "Not that I'm aware of."

"Good. What do you need then?"

Sean produced the receipt Felicity Pope had provided. "Can you pull up your security video around the time of this ticket?"

Willie glanced at it then turned toward the rear of the restaurant. "Sure, come on back."

Sean followed him through the wood-toned dining room and past the large horseshoe-shaped booths to a small office behind the kitchen. Willie pulled his keys, unlocked the door, and let them in. Sean shut the door behind them and waited while the manager cued up the video. A screen hanging above the desk came to life.

Examining the receipt, Willie twirled a control knob. "They sat at table fifty-two."

He punched in some numbers, which promptly produced the video Sean was in search of.

Sean pointed at the screen. "That's them, Willie."

As it played, they watched Felicity Pope and Monique Butler being seated then ordering drinks.

Their outfits matched what they had on when Sean first interviewed them at the station. He checked the timestamp in the lower corner of the playback—it aligned with the receipt. "Can I get a copy?"

Willie smiled. "You know you can. I'll have it sent over to the station."

"Perfect. The waitress on the video—who is that?"

"Carly."

"Is she here?"

"She comes in at four…" He looked at his watch. "Should be here any moment."

"Can I speak to her?"

"Sure."

Willie stood, leaving the picture frozen on the two women staring at their menus, and left the room. Moments later, he returned with a young woman dressed in a server's black Colonnade smock.

"Detective, this is Carly."

Sean smiled and shook her hand. "Hi, Carly. Would you mind taking a look at the picture on the screen?"

Her head rotated to look up at the wall.

"Do you remember those two women?"

She nodded. "Sure. Mother and daughter, I believe?"

"Good memory. Do you remember anything unusual about them?"

Carly's mouth turned down. "What do you mean by unusual?"

"Did they seem jittery or tense, maybe preoccupied?"

Her brow furrowed. "Nooo…not that I remember. They seemed nice enough, quite chatty, as I recall."

"Okay, thanks. That's all I needed."

Willie held the door for her. "Thanks, Carly."

When she was gone, Sean turned to the screen. "Let it play, will you?"

"Sure."

The video came to life again, and Sean watched the entirety of the women's meal. As Carly had said, they seemed chatty and comfortable. Of special interest to Sean, neither left the table nor took a phone call during the entire meal.

When they stood to leave, Sean checked the time again—three minutes before the ticket was stamped paid.

"Thanks, Willie."

"Anytime. You sure you won't stay for some catfish?"

"You know how to tempt a guy, but I'm afraid I can't. Work to do, but I'll take a rain check."

"You got it."

Sean headed back out through the dining room and into the afternoon sun. Once back in his car, he took out his phone, opened a stopwatch app, and started it. As the clock began to run, he pulled out of the parking lot and turned toward Collier Heights.

****

The 911 call from Monique Butler came in at just before eight Sunday night. Since Rodney Pope had been dead at least an hour when they called, they couldn't have been involved just prior to the call.

The ticket had them paying for their dinner at the Colonnade was stamped seven-twenty five.

Sean drove four different routes from the house to the restaurant, then back—a total of eight trips in all. He timed and logged each one. Regardless of which route he took or how much traffic he encountered, the trip was between twenty-nine and thirty four minutes.

Felicity Pope and Monique Butler arrived at the Colonnade just past six-thirty. That meant, for them to have killed Rodney Pope, they had to do it before six that night, and that was well outside the window given by Doc Carter.

Having just finished his last trip, Sean sat in his car and stared at the restaurant. No matter how he shaped it, the mother and daughter could not have physically carried out the killing. He'd spent nearly four hours driving back and forth to reach a conclusion that had seemed obvious already, but he had to eliminate them as the killers.

Problem is—who did I have left?

He'd yet to speak with Rodney Pope's girlfriend and his second wife. Maybe one of them could steer him in a new direction.

Yawning and rubbing his eyes, he decided sleep was in order, then he'd take a fresh run at things in the morning. He considered calling Mariah, but he'd been poor company the night before and would be worse tonight. Maybe calling her in the morning was a better idea.

Despite the biting cold air, he kept his car window open going home—just to make sure he was in bed *before* his eyes closed.

<u>Wednesday, December 20</u>

Atlanta Police Headquarters
Homicide Division
226 Peachtree Street SW
Downtown Atlanta
8:00 a.m.

Sean was up and out of the house on time. He called Mariah on the way to the precinct.

"Hello?"

"Good morning, you."

"Good morning, Sean. I missed you last night."

"I know, and I'm sorry, but I crashed out. I was beat. What did you do?"

"Mom, Sis, and I made Christmas cookies and watched *A Christmas Story.*"

"What about your dad? Did he watch it with you?"

She laughed. "No way. He raided the cookies before going to the basement and watching the basketball game."

"I might have joined him."

"What have you got against *A Christmas Story?*"

"It's all right, just not my favorite. Although, the first time I saw the duck's head chopped off, I nearly peed my pants!"

"You're sick."

"Yeah, and you love me. What's that say about you?"

"Good point. How's the case?"

91

He groaned. "About the same. Nothing solid to go on right now."

"Aww, keep after it. I have faith in you."

"Thank you kindly, madam. Your confidence is appreciated."

"By the way, did you hear?"

"Evidently not."

"They're saying it could be a white Christmas!" She sounded giddy.

"No kidding?"

"Wouldn't that be cool? The last white Christmas was in 1881."

He laughed. "Over a hundred years ago! You know what that tells me?"

"What?"

"Don't hold your breath."

"Oh, you! Don't be a Scrooge."

"You're right. I'm sorry." He pulled into the station parking lot. "Gotta run. Love you."

"Love you more."

"Not possible."

When he got to his desk, a note was waiting for him.

Pope Funeral
H.M. Patterson
Spring Hill Chapel
4:00 P.M.

Sean, like almost all investigators, made a point to attend the funeral of their victim, not only to pay his respects but to watch the people who attended. More than one case had been solved with information gleaned at the solemn ceremony.

Sean wanted to be there as an investigator, but he also wanted the family to know he hadn't forgotten them. He was still here for them and still working to find justice for their loved one. At a time like that, symbolism was very important—and many times said more than what words could convey.

He tucked the note into his pocket and sat down at his desk. He'd expected to brief Lieutenant Mitchell, but her office was empty. Maybe he could make his first appointment and get out before she showed up.

Sean checked his notes and found the phone number for Sally Robinson, then dialed.

"Hello?"

"Sally Robinson, please."

"Speaking."

"Miss Robinson, this is Detective Sparks with the Atlanta police department."

A brief moment of silence. "I guess I knew you'd call. This is about Rodney, isn't it?"

"Yes, ma'am."

"What can I do for you, Detective?"

"I'd like to visit with you. Is there a convenient time we could talk?"

"Well…I go into work at one. You can come now if you'd like."

"That would be perfect. You're on Collier Drive, correct?"

"Yes. Number 3083."

"I'll be there shortly."

He hung up, then using Division of Driver Services records, he located a number for a Natalie Dennis in Marietta. He dialed, and as the phone rang, it dawned on him that she might not have been notified of her ex-husband's death.

"Hello?" A male voice came over the phone.

"Natalie Dennis, please."

"One minute."

Silently, Sean hoped she'd found out somehow.

"Hello."

"Mrs. Dennis?"

"That's right. Who's this?"

"Ma'am, my name is Detective Sparks. I'm with the Atlanta police department."

"Detective? Why would you need to speak to me?"

Sean's heart sank. "Mrs. Dennis, it's in relation to your ex-husband, Rodney Pope."

"Rodney! Surely, he's not in trouble."

"Ma'am, I'm sorry to have to tell you this, but…Mr. Pope was killed Saturday."

She sucked in a deep breath. "Killed? Rodney's *dead*?"

"Yes, ma'am. I'm afraid so."

"What happened?"

"He was murdered."

"I…I…I don't know what to say. Who would want to kill Rodney?"

"That's what I'm trying to find out. May I come by and see you?"

"I'm in Marietta."

"Yes, ma'am. I'd still like to drive up and speak with you."

John C. Dalglish

There was a hesitation and the sound of muffled voices. Sean waited.

"Detective...Sparks, did you say?"

"Yes, ma'am."

"I'll be home this afternoon if that works for you."

"That will be fine. One-thirty, maybe?"

"My husband will be here. I assume that's okay."

"No problem. I have your address as 226 Oakridge Drive. Is that correct?"

"It is. We're due west of Dobbins Air Base, if you know where that is."

"I do. Thank you, and I'll see you this afternoon."

He hung up and headed for the parking lot. Marietta was about an hour north of Atlanta, so he should have no trouble getting back in time for the funeral. Suddenly, his day had gotten very full, which he hadn't anticipated when he'd first woke up that morning. It was almost a relief.

It beats staring at the case file and rubbing my chin!

Home of Sally Robinson
3083 Collier Drive
Collier Heights Neighborhood
9:45 a.m.

On the way to Sally Robinson's address, Sean passed by Dr. Mary Shy Scott Memorial Park. Out of curiosity, he wheeled into the parking lot and checked the surroundings.

95

This was where Rodney Pope would park and walk to Miss Robinson's home.

The tiny gravel lot could hold just a handful of cars, and it couldn't be more than a quarter mile to Sally's front door. He turned around and went back out onto Collier Drive, drove for less than a minute, then turned into the long driveway that led up to Miss Robinson's house.

The low-slung stucco structure was almost completely encompassed by trees and shrubs, concealing the pale-pink exterior from the road. White rod iron supported a small carport and entranceway. He parked and got out.

Even though a cold wind swept across the lawn, the front door was open, and only the glass storm door shielded the interior of the home. Sean tapped on the glass.

"Just a minute!"

Sally Robinson shuffled down the hallway toward the door and unsnapped the lock. "Detective Sparks, I gather."

"Yes, ma'am."

"Please come in."

Sean gladly came in out of the wind. The trees that shaded the house in summer had dropped their leaves, but the thick woods still made the interior of the home dark. He paused while Miss Robinson flipped on the hall light then moved around him.

"Would you like to sit down, Detective?"

"If you don't mind."

"Certainly. Come back to the kitchen."

Sean followed her down the hallway and into a small kitchen. A table and two chairs filled the tiny dining area, and low cabinets that divided the cooking area from the table and chairs hung from the ceiling, which served to shrink the room further—almost to the point of claustrophobic.

She pointed at one of the chairs. "Please, make yourself comfortable. Would you like something to drink?"

"No, thank you. I'm fine."

She wore a rose-colored paisley smock and pink house slippers. Sitting opposite him, she sipped her glass of water then folded her hands in her lap and waited.

Sean took out his notepad. "Thank you for seeing me."

"Of course."

It wasn't until he met her gaze that he realized her eyes were moist and bloodshot. She'd been crying. "I'm sorry for your loss, Miss Robinson."

"Thank you."

"How long had you and Mr. Pope been seeing each other?"

"A little over a year. We met walking at Scott Park. At first, we would just walk together, but before long, it became more than that."

"I understand Mr. Pope would walk over here every evening. Is that correct?"

"It is. Rodney was stuck in a bad situation, but he and I were willing to be patient until things were resolved. He would come by for dinner then return home."

Sean made a note. "Could you describe your relationship with Mr. Pope?"

"In a word—wonderful." She lifted her glass, sipped it again, then returned it to the same spot on the table. "Rodney was loving, respectful, kind… I miss him."

"Did Mr. Pope confide in you about the situation between him and his wife?"

"Of course. I knew she was being terrible to him."

"She?"

"Felicity. She was doing her best to make his life miserable."

Sean wasn't about to take her comments at face value, but she seemed genuine in her affection for Rodney Pope.

"Did he describe the situation in detail?"

"You mean, did he tell me he was afraid of her?"

Sean nodded, concealing his surprise.

"Just a few weeks ago, he told me he was locking himself in his bedroom at night. Does that answer your question?"

"It does." He paused, considering how to broach the next topic. "Did Mr. Pope discuss his finances with you?"

"Did we talk about money?"

"Yes."

"I know he wasn't happy about her trying to keep his share of the house. I'm guessing that's what you're referring to."

"What about with you? Did he ever borrow money?"

"Rodney? Please." Her tone was mocking. "Rodney was generous to a fault. He even insisted on paying for the groceries I bought for our dinners." She lifted the glass to her lips again, this time holding it up and looking over the top at him. "Rodney Pope was a good man, and I loved him very much. Money had nothing to do with it."

Sean met her gaze. "I have to ask. Where were you Sunday night, Miss Robinson?"

She sighed. "Here. After Rodney left…"

"What time was that?"

"Just about seven, I believe. Anyway, I did the dishes, watched some TV, then turned in around nine."

Sean folded up his notepad. "Again, I'm very sorry for your loss."

She took a long drink of water. When she pulled the glass away from her face, her eyes had filled with tears. "Detective?"

"Ma'am?"

"Do you know when the funeral is?"

"Yes. It's this afternoon at four."

"Are you going?"

"I plan to."

"Could you do me a favor?"

"I'll try."

"Obviously, I can't go…but…would you go up to the casket and tell Rodney I'll be thinking of him?"

Sean hesitated, working to choke back his emotions. "I can do that."

"Somehow, I want Rodney to know I would have been there if possible." Tears rolled down her face. "And when he's laid to rest, please let me know where. I want to visit him."

Sean's face flushed. "I…I'll be certain to let you know."

"Thank you."

Sean stood unsteadily. "I'll let myself out."

"Goodbye, Detective."

"Goodbye, Miss Robinson."

Sean walked out into the cold wind. It chilled his tear-covered cheeks. The love displayed by Sally Robinson was so genuine, it reminded him of an old George Strait song. *I Saw God Today…*

Sean hurried to his car, anxious to get on the move.

If Henderson had cautioned him once, he'd warned Sean a thousand times. "Try not to get emotionally involved while working a case. There's time for that *after* you've gotten justice for the family."

But Henderson had always followed it up with another statement. "Nearly impossible, but try."

Home of Natalie Dennis
226 Oakridge Drive
Marietta, Ga
1:15 p.m.

Sean grabbed a burger and ate on the highway as he drove up to Marietta, a city of roughly fifty thousand people. Its largest employer, next to the school system, was the Lockheed Martin Aerospace plant.

Sean had been to the city on numerous occasions, many of which involved the *Big Chicken*—a fifty-six foot tall steel chicken attached to the front of a KFC. Whenever visitors came into Atlanta, they would invariably ask Sean to take them up for a look.

He'd once seen a t-shirt bearing photos of the Eiffel Tower, Big Ben, the Roman Coliseum, and the Big Chicken. Some reports said pilots approaching Hartsfield-Jackson airport in Atlanta used the giant structure as a reference point, and there was even a barbershop quartet name the *Big Chicken Chorus.*

To Sean, it was kind of freaky and had giant eyes that moved. Today, his trip would not take him by the creepy fowl. He pulled into the driveway of the Dennis home fifteen minutes ahead of schedule.

After getting out of the car and stretching, he crossed the huge front lawn to get to the tiny house. He estimated the little place with its white vinyl siding and brown shutters to be no more than eight hundred square feet.

As he stepped onto the front stoop, the door opened to reveal a fit woman in her late sixties wearing a black pant suit. Her gray hair was cut to collar length and swept across her forehead to one side.

She smiled politely. "Detective Sparks?"

Sean showed his badge. "Yes, ma'am."

"Come in out of that wind."

"Thank you."

He was let into the living room, from which he could see the entire rest of the home. A bathroom was off to his left, and the small kitchen sat diagonal from where he stood. Next to the bathroom door were two other doors, which Sean assumed were bedrooms. Though it was small, it was not crowded since the furniture seemed to have been selected with the size of the room in mind.

Natalie Dennis swept her arm toward the man sitting on the loveseat. "That is my husband, Vince Dennis."

The man lifted himself up and gripped Sean's hand in an iron-strong handshake. "Nice to meet you, Detective."

"Likewise, sir."

Mrs. Dennis pulled a pillow off of an armchair, freeing up the space for Sean. "Please, make yourself comfortable. Would you like something to drink?"

Sean held up a hand. "No, thanks."

She lowered herself gracefully onto the loveseat and took her husband's hand. "I was shocked to hear about Rodney."

"I'm sorry for dropping it on you like that. I had hoped you may have heard from some other source. I know a phone call from a detective is a hard way to learn of a dear one's death."

She gave him a sad smile. "I'm sure it's no easier to deliver the news. How can I help?"

He tucked his badge away and extracted his notepad. "Mrs. Dennis, I understand you were married to Mr. Pope for ten years. Is that accurate?"

"Yes."

"Could you describe your relationship for me?"

"Well, it was good most of the time. Rodney was a kind and generous man."

"May I ask how the divorce came about?"

"He was gone a lot as a member of the Coast Guard. I grew lonely and eventually, a little resentful. Rodney tried to get transferred nearer to my parents, but by the time the move was granted, we had grown apart."

"So the divorce was mutual?"

"Mutual and amicable."

"Were there any issues in the marriage over money?"

The question sounded crass, even to Sean, but Natalie Dennis accepted it with grace.

"What married couples don't squabble about finances? Most of the time, if we argued over money, it was because Rodney had helped a friend and left us a little short. He did that kind of thing all the time."

Sean had heard this story before. "When was the last time you spoke with Mr. Pope?"

"Gosh, I don't know." She glanced at her husband.

Vince Dennis smiled. "Don't look at me; I haven't a clue."

"Oh, you." She patted his knee. "It's been years, I guess."

"So, you probably can't think of anyone who would want to hurt Mr. Pope."

She paused. "You know something, I can't remember anyone being angry enough with Rodney to even yell at him."

"Forgive me, but I have to ask where you were last Sunday night."

She dismissed the question with a wave. "You're doing your job; we understand. Vince and I were at church for Sunday evening singing. In fact…" She rotated in her seat and lifted a piece of paper off the side table. "This is the program."

Sean accepted it and glanced quickly at the date and time. "May I keep this?"

"Of course."

He put away his pad. "I appreciate your time. I guess I don't have any other questions."

"I'm sorry you had to drive up here just for that. I wish I could be more help."

"Actually, you've been very helpful."

She stood and led him to the door. He handed her his card. "If you think of anything, please call."

"I certainly will."

Sean nodded at Vince Dennis. "Good-day, sir."

Back outside, Sean pulled his collar up against the wind as he made his way back across the wide lawn. He got into his car and stared at the little house.

The people in Rodney Pope's life all seemed to love the man—except his soon-to-be ex-wife Felicity. Problem was, she had an alibi, not to mention she didn't seem physically capable of bashing the life out of a man with a blunt object.

Dead ends! That's all I've got!

There has to be somebody who didn't like this guy enough to kill him.

A rather obvious thought.

Unless it was the most difficult type of murder a detective could face—a stranger killing—not a path he was anxious to go down yet. He started the car.

For the moment, his priority was to keep a promise.

Young Funeral Home
1107 Hank Aaron Drive SW
South Atlanta
4:10 p.m.

Sean was few minutes late getting to the large, antebellum structure that was Young Funeral Home. An expansive porch ran across the front, and though it had rocking chairs for visitors, the blustery, overcast skies had forced everyone inside.

He parked on the street, and taking the concrete steps two at a time, he made it inside as music began playing from the chapel. An usher was just getting ready to close the doors but hesitated when he saw Sean. Slipping into the nearest wood pew, he scanned the scene in front of him.

Not surprisingly, considering the injuries Mr. Pope had suffered, the silver-rimmed casket was closed. Behind it, on an easel, sat a large photo of Rodney Pope. Dressed in a blue pinstripe suit, the man in the picture reminded Sean of the CEO of some company, serious looking but pleasant.

Felicity Pope and Monique Butler were in the front row, accompanied by a man Sean didn't recognize. All three sat directly in front of the portrait, which was surrounded by a large number of flowers that overflowed the podium to either side. Rodney Pope seemed almost to be staring down at the two women.

The pews were nearly full, many of the attendees wiping their eyes. Sean had been to more funerals than he cared to remember, and all funerals were solemn occasions, but the atmosphere at this one was especially oppressive. Apparently, Rodney Pope would be missed by a lot of people.

The service ran nearly an hour. Testimonials were given by various people who, when the floor was opened up, stood to reminisce about their friend and colleague. A pastor, presumably from Felicity and Rodney's church, gave the eulogy. Neither Monique nor Felicity spoke, but that was hardly a surprise.

Meet me at the cross played as the service ended, and a line of people began greeting Felicity and her daughter, bending to say a few words then moving on. Sean remained seated until the last of the mourners were in line then got up and went forward.

Stopping next to the casket, he laid his hand on it and looked up at the photo of Mr. Pope. Under his breath, he kept his promise.

"Sally sends her love, Mr. Pope." He swallowed hard as he pictured Sally Robinson. "She wants you to know she's here in spirit and won't forget you."

When he turned around, Monique was staring at him. He pretended not to notice and approached with his hand extended. "I'm sorry for your loss."

She accepted the physical contact as if she feared he had leprosy. "Thank you."

The gentleman who had been sitting with her was gone. Sean opted not to question the ladies about him—not here.

Felicity Pope looked up. "Detective Sparks. Thank you for coming."

"It's my honor to be here. I'm so sorry."

She averted her eyes. Despite the state of her relationship with Rodney, she still seemed to be genuinely grieving his death. "It's been a tough few days, obviously."

"Is there going to be a graveside ceremony?"

"Rodney wanted to be cremated. We'll be interring his ashes at Westview Cemetery tomorrow morning."

"Privately, I gather."

She nodded. "Is there any news about who did this to him?"

"I'm afraid not. But I promise you I'm doing my best to find out."

"Thank you, Detective."

Sean turned to Monique and found her watching him. "Miss Butler, would you be able to come by and see me tomorrow afternoon?"

John C. Dalglish

Monique's mouth turned downward. "I…I suppose."

"I would appreciate it. Just give me a call and let me know what time is good for you."

"Very well."

Sean stepped back and started toward the exit. Something nagged at him, and he had almost reached his car when it suddenly dawned on him—both women had dry eyes. Of all the people at the service, they seemed the most likely to be emotional. Then again, considering the acrimony between Rodney and Felicity, maybe it wasn't that big a surprise after all.

Still…

Back in his car, he drew in a long breath then dialed the number for Sally Robinson.

"Hello?"

"Miss Robinson, it's Detective Sparks."

Her voice trembled. "Yes, Detective."

"I just left the service." His voice quivered. "Rodney…he knows you were thinking of him."

A long pause. "Thank you, Detective."

"Call me Sean."

"Thank you, Sean."

He was about to hang up when he remembered his other task. "Oh…"

"Yes?"

"His ashes will be buried tomorrow morning at Westview Cemetery."

"I know where that is. God bless you. Your kindness means a lot."

"It was my honor, ma'am. Goodnight."

"Goodnight, Sean."

He hung up and laid his phone on the seat. The gray sky matched his mood, and without anything pressing to follow up on, he headed for home.

Hopefully, Mariah could come by.

Home of Detective Sean Sparks
Camden Vantage Apartments
Sweet Auburn Neighborhood
East of Downtown Atlanta
6:05 p.m.

The number one thing Sean loved to do for relaxation was cook—especially for others—and he took pride in his culinary skills. Creating a meal served as an escape from work because it required him to concentrate. If he allowed himself to become distracted, he'd likely burn something or add too much seasoning, both of which were unacceptable.

He'd stopped on the way home to pick up the ingredients for his homemade jambalaya, one of Mariah's absolute favorites. He would make enough for her to take some home to her mom and dad. Sean had grown very close to Mariah's family, and they loved his food as much as their daughter did.

Mariah would be over around seven, so he got busy cooking.

After sautéing the chicken and andouille sausage, he set them aside and chopped the vegetables. Onion, green pepper, celery, garlic, and fresh tomatoes went into his version, along with rice, chicken broth, and Worcestershire sauce for flavor. He then made it spicy—adding in red pepper flakes and hot pepper sauce for heat—just the way Mariah liked it.

The pot was simmering on the stove when she arrived.

"Hey!"

"In here."

She padded into the kitchen and kissed his check, her lips still cold from being outside. "Ooh, is that what I think it is?"

"If you think it's jambalaya, then yes."

"Of course! Nothing on Earth smells as good as your concoction."

"No need to butter me up. You'll get some."

She wrapped her arms around his neck and pouted. "I've missed you so."

He kissed her pouty lips. "I've missed you, too."

"How's the case?"

He held his hand up. "Nope! No work talk."

"Okay!" She let go and went to the fridge. "You won't get any argument from me. Want a beer?"

"Sure."

She handed him one and opened hers. "I know what we should talk about instead."

He took a long sip then leaned against the counter. "Oh, really?"

"My Christmas present."

"Your present? Why would we talk about that?"

"*Well...*" She practically purred the word as she slinked across the kitchen floor. "I thought maybe you might want some ideas."

"No, I don't think so."

She stopped short, and the pout returned. "Why not?"

He shrugged. "I'm on top of it."

She put a hand on her hip and cocked her head to one side. "Oh, really! I know you—you'll wait until the last possible moment."

"Maybe you don't know me as well as you think."

A Cheshire cat smile curled her lips. "What is it?"

"I'm not telling you that."

"Fine. What about a hint?"

"Oh, no. Not a single clue. You can wait like all the other good kiddos in the world."

She pretended to be upset, but her eyes twinkled and gave away her delight.

He set his beer down and lifted the lid on the food. "Let's do a flavor test."

After scooping some out with a spoon, he held it over his hand for her to sip.

She slurped it and grinned. "Mmmmm!"

He replaced the lid. "So, you don't like it."

She scoffed. "Yeah, it's terrible. When do we eat?"

He laughed. "Soon. Now, come over here and tell me again how much you love me."

"I don't remember saying so for the first time yet."

"Then tell me for the first time, then tell me again."

She smiled and kissed him. "I love you."

"Love you more."

"Not possible."

John C. Dalglish

Thursday, December 21

Atlanta Police Headquarters
Homicide Division
226 Peachtree Street SW
Downtown Atlanta
7:30 a.m.

With nothing solid to go on that morning, Sean's first task was to prepare warrants—lots of them. Phone and financials records on the victim Mr. Pope, Felicity Pope, and Monique Butler. What exactly he was after, he didn't know. It was like a fishing expedition—sometimes, you don't know where the big ones were hiding until you cast your net—and Sean was using the biggest net he could find.

After gathering up his forms, he went to Lieutenant Mitchell's office and tapped on the closed door.

"Come!"

He jumped a little then laughed self-consciously. How could such a classy lady have such a brassy voice?

It was like being summoned by Bette Midler!

He pushed the door partway open. "Got a minute, Lieutenant?"

"Sparks. Perfect. Come in."

He did, shutting the door behind him before dropping into the nearest seat.

111

Mitchell pointed at her phone. "I'm just off the line with Monique Butler. She wants to know if we can release her mother's house. Can we?"

He shrugged. "If forensics doesn't need it, I don't think I will."

"Good. Let her know, okay?"

"I have a meeting with her today, so I'll tell her then." He laid a sheath of papers on his boss's desk.

She stared at the pile. "What have we here?"

"Warrants. I want to flesh out the main characters fully."

She pulled them toward her and rifled through them. "Okay. No problem. Got a lead on one of them?"

"Not really. The two women have solid alibis, but…"

"But what?"

Sean shrugged. "Due diligence, I suppose… I don't know. In all my interviews with people who knew Rodney Pope, the only one who seemed to have an issue with him was the widow, Felicity Pope. She and Rodney were in a contentious divorce, and her distaste for the victim was palpable."

"But she has a solid alibi, correct?"

"Yes, ma'am."

"Then what are you after?"

"Evidence of conspiracy." Sean surprised himself with the statement. He hadn't yet formed the whole picture in his own head, never mind verbalized it.

Mitchell tipped back in her chair and regarded him with narrowed eyes. "A contract killing?"

He nodded.

"Sean, a stranger killing is rare. Do you know what type of murder is even rarer?"

He did now. "A paid hit?"

"In all the years I've worked homicide, I've never worked a murder-for-hire case."

"Really?"

She nodded. "Obviously, I've heard about them and even studied a few, but I've never had one personally."

Sean began to doubt the idea. Perhaps he was grasping at straws. "Obviously, I was unaware."

She sighed. "Look, I'm not saying you're on the wrong track, and I'm going to sign your warrants because they're something you need to cover, but…"

He waited, a sense of dread creeping in.

"Even though murder for hire is the rarest case type, it's not the most difficult. We both know that a stranger-on-stranger killing is the toughest to solve, and the most common to go cold, but…"

Crap! Another but.

"Don't avoid going down that path if it's where the evidence leads you."

So there it was. She thought he was taking the easy way out. Maybe she suspected him of stalling until Henderson could be sprung free and come to his rescue.

Is that the truth? Am I having the detective's version of cold feet?

Mitchell was watching him, and he sensed what he said next would go a long way in determining his future with *her* homicide department.

"You have my word, Lieutenant; I'll go where the evidence leads and consider any theory, as long as the facts support it."

She held his gaze for a few seconds longer, then nodded quickly. "Good. That's all I ask. I'll sign these and get them processed."

Sean stood. "Thank you."

He turned for the door.

"Sean?"

He looked back. "Ma'am."

"You wouldn't be lead on a case in my department if I didn't think you had what it takes. Understand?"

"Yes, ma'am."

"Good. Dismissed."

Sean went back to his desk. The hair on his neck prickled, as if everyone in the squad room was looking at him, but a glance around told him he was just being paranoid. He wasn't sure what to think. On one hand, she'd questioned his premise on the case, then on the other, she'd given him a serious compliment.

Maybe that's her point. She wants you to prove yourself to yourself—not to her.

Then again, maybe he was just overthinking it.

Interview Room 4
Atlanta Police Headquarters
226 Peachtree Street SW
Downtown Atlanta
2:30 p.m.

Shortly after meeting with the lieutenant, Sean received a call from Monique Butler. He delivered the news that her mother could retake possession of her home. Monique then asked for time to arrange a cleaning service before coming down for her interview at one-thirty. He said that was fine, but she was late.

When he showed her into interview room 4, she took the chair he offered but didn't mention the fact she was late. Sean had his recorder, which he clicked on.

"I'm Detective Sparks, and with me is Monique Butler. The date is the twenty-first of December, and the time is 2:35 p.m." He opened the folder he had brought with him. "Miss Butler, you're here voluntarily, correct?"

"Correct."

"Thank you for coming down."

"Of course, Detective. Anything to help."

"I need to get a little background first. Have you ever been married?"

"No, never been that unlucky."

She smiled, but Sean wasn't sure she was joking.

"Are you currently dating anyone?"

"Yes, Bill Ashton. Why is that important?"

"Just background." He met her gaze. "He wouldn't happen to be the man sitting with you at the funeral?"

"As a matter of fact, yes."

"Does Mr. Ashton live in Savannah, also?"

"He does. He drives for Atlantic Coast Freight out of the Port of Savannah."

Sean's interest increased. "How long have you been dating?"

"Almost a year, I believe."

"Do you happen to know where he was Sunday night?"

Monique crossed her arms and sighed. "You'll have to ask him. He was on a long haul."

"Could I have his number?"

She recited it from memory.

Sean switched channels. "When did you get to town?"

"I came in last Friday."

"Was it a planned visit?"

She frowned. "What do you mean by planned?"

"Well…was it spur of the moment, or had you made the plans to come a few weeks ago."

"It wasn't spur of the moment, but I didn't expect to come up here until Christmas Eve."

"I see. So what changed your plans?"

She stared directly at him, shifting slightly in her seat, and her eyes welled up. "I was worried about Mom."

"Her health?"

"You could say that."

"I'm afraid I don't understand."

A tissue suddenly appeared from her purse, and she dabbed at her eyes. "Have you ever known someone who committed suicide, Detective?"

"No, ma'am, I haven't."

"It is the most tragic of deaths because it is almost always preventable."

"Are you suggesting your mother was considering suicide?"

The tissue disappeared. "My mother has gone through a lot with the disintegration of her marriage. She acts as if she doesn't care, but I believe she blames herself for losing her relationship with Rodney. As Christmas approached, her

John C. Dalglish

comments became more and more dark. I worried she might do something foolish."

"To who?"

"To herself."

Sean had seen both sides of the depression coin. Sometimes, the sadness turned to anger that festered then was turned toward the person they blamed for the pain. The other and more common result in cases of domestic abuse was to see the victim turn the damage inward, blaming themselves. Not that Felicity had been abused—she'd never made such a claim—but she may carry the burden Monique had described.

"Did you find your worries valid when you arrived?"

"I did, at least, I think my arrival pulled her out of a dark place—until Sunday night, of course."

"Of course."

Sean began to consider his contract killing theory in a new light. Monique Butler was caring and open—not the attributes of a murderer.

"I think I have everything I need. Thank you for coming down."

"It was no problem, Detective." She stood and moved toward the door. "By the way, thank you for releasing the house. Mom needs a familiar environment right now, even with what took place there."

"Give her my best."

"I will. Good day."

Sean gathered his notes and his recorder then headed back to his desk. He needed to confirm that Bill Ashton was nowhere near the Pope home on Sunday night, then he could move on. To what, he wasn't sure.

****

It was just before five when Sean got ahold of Bill Ashton.

"Hello?"

"Mr. Bill Ashton, please."

"This is he."

"Mr. Ashton, I'm Detective Sparks with Atlanta PD."

"Yes, Monique mentioned you might call."

This time, Sean didn't mind that potential person of interest had tipped off another. Either Ashton had an alibi, or he didn't. "Sir, I'm trying to establish your location this past Sunday night. I understand you were on the road."

"That's right. I dropped a load in Buffalo, New York Saturday morning and secured a new load in Rochester Saturday evening. I left out of Rochester Sunday morning early."

"How long a trip is that?"

"Generally, about fifteen hours, but I had to lay over per driving rules. I laid over in Fayetteville, North Carolina Sunday night and got back into Savannah Monday."

"I see. Are you a solo or team driver?"

He grunted. "Solo. I don't trust anyone but myself in one of these rigs."

"I understand. Is your truck equipped with company monitored GPS?"

"Of course."

Sean had what he needed. "Thank you for your time, sir."

"Sure."

Sean hung up just as a pile of papers landed on his desk. He looked up at the uniformed officer delivering them.

The officer smiled. "Phone records."

"Thanks."

Sean ignored them for the moment and looked up the number for Atlantic Coast Freight. A pleasant female voice picked up on the second ring.

"A-C-F. How can I direct your call?"

"My name is Detective Sparks with Atlanta PD. I need to speak with someone about a driver's location. Who would that be?"

"I imagine dispatch could do that. Please hold."

As was common in Georgia, hold music was often from homegrown musicians that had made it big in country music such as Luke Bryan, Jason Alden, or Trisha Yearwood. This time, Alan Jackson serenaded Sean while he waited.

"Dispatch."

"Yes, my name is Detective Sparks with the Atlanta Police Department. I need to verify the whereabouts of one of your drivers this past Sunday night."

The male voice was friendly but guarded. "I'll need your badge number, Detective."

Sean recited it.

"Thank you. Which driver?"

"Bill Ashton."

A keyboard clicked multiple times in Sean's ear.

"I'm afraid exact information of the truck's whereabouts is private company data. Without a warrant, I can only give you a general location."

"That's all I need at this time."

"From seven-thirty Sunday evening until six in the morning Monday, Mr. Ashton's truck was in the general area of Fayetteville, North Carolina."

Mr. Ashton's truck?

"What about him personally? Does he have to check in?"

"No, and the GPS is on his truck. I can't speak for him personally."

"I understand. Thank you for your help."

Sean hung up and opened his laptop. Doing a quick search of a Fayetteville to Atlanta road trip, he checked the time. To reach Atlanta, commit the murder, then return to Fayetteville would take almost twelve hours under perfect conditions. No way could Ashton make the trip and be back on the road at six in the morning. Unless someone else drove the semi for him, his alibi checked out.

Sean stared at the pile of phone records. It was going to be a long night. He pushed himself up and went to fill his coffee cup.

<u>Friday, December 22</u>

Atlanta Police Headquarters
Homicide Division
226 Peachtree Street SW
Downtown Atlanta
8:10 a.m.

Sean didn't leave the precinct until well after midnight but dragged himself out of bed and got back in early. He nursed a cup of coffee while considering what he'd learned from his late-night study session of the phone records. Bottom line? *Not much.*

In fact, the call logs only managed to strengthen further the conclusion that neither Felicity Pope nor Monique Butler had anything to do with Rodney Pope's murder. All the phone numbers were easily accounted for, and none of the calls they'd made or received seemed to last inordinately long or be repetitive enough to suggest a plot.

The only number Sean could not identify right away, and had to run a check on, turned out to be Monique's ex-husband—who Sean intended to talk with as soon as possible. Still, with only three calls between them over a period of two weeks, it seemed unlikely at best that they were planning something as serious as a murder.

The phone on his desk rang, breaking his concentration. He snatched it up.

"Homicide—Detective Sparks."

121

"Good morning, Detective. This is Tom Bradley. I was the responding officer on the Pope murder."

"Yes, Tom. I remember."

"I made an arrest last night that I thought you should know about."

"Okay. Why's that?"

"At around eleven p.m., I had a call regarding a burglary in progress. When I arrived at the address, I discovered an individual leaving the back of the home. After a short pursuit, I was able to apprehend him."

Sean realized he was drumming his fingers on the desk. "I see."

"Anyway, he entered the residence by breaking a window with a bat."

The finger drumming stopped, and Sean's heart started pounding. "A baseball bat?"

"Yes."

"Was he carrying it at the time?"

"He was."

"Where did this happen?"

"On Cedar Avenue in Center Hill."

Sean's mental map zoomed in on the location. "That's just east of Collier Heights, isn't it?"

"Yes, sir. I'd had a chance to read the crime scene report on the Pope case—call it curiosity—and I saw the reference to a bat."

"Did you notice anything else that seemed to fit?"

"Actually, yes. We located the suspect's vehicle just a block away from the break-in. He had several laptops in the trunk."

Sean's adrenaline surged. "What was the suspect's name?"

"Terrance Lee."

"Does he have a record?"

"He does not, sir."

The fact that Lee had no record came as *good* news. His prints wouldn't be on file, meaning his thumb might still match the print pulled from the plastic casino mug that had contained the stolen money.

"Where is he now?"

"In county."

"And the bat?"

"Both it and the laptops were taken for processing to the GBI lab."

"Thank you for the heads up, Tom. You're welcome to read my case notes anytime."

Bradley laughed. "Okay. Bye."

Sean hung up and dialed Tasha King at GBI headquarters.

"Forensics."

"Tasha King, please."

"One moment."

She came on quickly. "This is Agent King."

"Hi, Tasha. It's Sean Sparks."

"Good morning, Sean. How's it going?"

"Okay. You?"

"Busy. What can I do for you?"

Sean glanced at his notes. "A Terrance Lee was booked into county last night. Can you look up his prints and compare them to the unidentified one from the plastic mug in my Pope case?"

"Sure. I'll get it done this morning."

"Thanks, I appreciate it."

"No problem. Anything else?"

"Actually, yes. A baseball bat and some laptops were sent to your lab for processing. I'm wondering if blood was found on the bat. It could be my murder weapon."

"Okay, I'll see who's doing the evaluation and give them a heads up."

"I'm also in search of a stolen laptop. Maybe I'll come by later and look those over myself."

"No problem."

"Thanks again, Tasha. Bye."

Sean hung up and headed for his car.

Fulton County Jail
901 Rice St NW,
North of Downtown Atlanta
9:45 a.m.

If you saw the Fulton County Jail from above, it would look like two of those wind spinners you held as a kid and blew on to make them turn, only made of beige brick instead of multi-colored plastic. Standing outside the jail, it resembled two ten-story apartment buildings with funny-looking windows. A large, square buttress anchored by a modern glass entryway joined the two structures.

Sean parked in the public lot and used the main entrance. After checking in and passing through the security door, he arranged to have Terrance Lee brought to an interview suite.

Suite was far too kind a description for the seven-foot square room with dull cement walls, three hardback chairs, and a table fastened to the floor. The inmate's chair faced the back wall and the video camera, which recorded everything in the room.

While he waited for Lee to be brought from the jail, Sean studied the driver's license photo on file with the Division of Driver Services.

Lee, clearly of Asian descent, had a round face and a stare that challenged you to cross him. His picture came across as threatening, which didn't mesh with the fact he didn't have a record. Still, it was just a DDS picture, and Lee wouldn't be the first to have a bad photo taken there.

The door opened, and Lee, wearing the standard blue smock and blue pants of the Fulton County Jail, was escorted into the room by a sheriff's deputy. The deputy undid the cuffs and waited until Lee was seated.

Sean smiled at the young man. "Would you like something to drink, Terrance?"

"Yeah, a Coke."

Sean looked up at the deputy. "Would you mind?"

The deputy nodded and left the room.

Sean took out his notepad. "So, Terrance—"

"T-roe."

Sean looked up. "That's what your friends call you?"

"Yeah."

The deputy re-entered with a can of Coke and set it in front of Lee.

Sean nodded. "Thank you. We'll be fine."

The deputy stepped outside, closing the door behind him.

"So, T-roe, my name is Detective Sparks."

The young man shrugged, popped open the soda, and took a sip.

Sean sized up the person before him. Heavy, probably two hundred and fifty pounds or more, he hardly fit the profile of a stealth burglar. "I gather this jail thing is a new experience for you."

Lee locked eyes with Sean and seemed unphased by his situation. "Never been caught before if that's what you mean. I got sloppy."

"I see. So, this wasn't your first burglary."

"Maybe… Maybe not."

"Are you curious why I wanted to talk to you?"

"I figured it had to do with that stuff someone left in my car."

"Left in your car?" Sean smiled. "Who was this person?"

Another shrug. "Must have been someone from my apartment complex." A little smile curled the edges of Lee's mouth. "They probably ditched the stuff."

"That stuff, as you call it, is stolen merchandise, and some of it may be tied to a case I'm working."

"Stolen? I didn't know that."

This kid was too cool for someone who'd never been arrested. Sean guessed there was a juvenile record somewhere that a judge had sealed. Either way, it was time to wipe the smile off T-roe's face.

"That's right, and what you'll find really interesting is the case I'm working—it's a murder."

The can, halfway to his mouth, froze in place. "Murder! I ain't committed no murder."

Sean sighed. "You know what's funny, Terrance?"

"I said to call me T-roe."

Sean ignored the outburst. "What's funny is this. If one of those laptops in your possession comes back to my victim, you're looking at a murder rap."

Lee's eyes widened with fear. "I told you—those aren't my laptops!"

"I know that, Terrance. They were stolen."

"Okay, maybe. But I didn't kill nobody."

"So you said." Sean glanced down at his notes. "Where were you last Sunday night?"

Lee set his Coke down and scrunched his forehead. "Uh…let's see. I was with my girlfriend."

"Let me guess—the two of you went to church."

Lee shook his head. "We went to my nephew's birthday party."

"Okay. What time was the party?"

"Seven."

"And where was this party?"

"Westhaven."

"The address, Terrance."

"2855 Burton."

Sean placed it in his mental map. Westhaven was the neighborhood directly south of Collier Heights. "What's your girlfriend's name and number?"

"Jasmine Sanders." He gave Sean the number from memory. "And the party was at my sister's house. Her name is April Roy."

Sean wrote down her number, as well. "I'm going to check this all out, Terrance. It better be on the level, or you're in a world of trouble. If you're feeding me a line, it will make things worse for you."

"I swear, man! I never killed no one."

Sean folded his pad and put it away. He got up and opened the door. "He's ready to go back."

Lee drained the rest of his soda before allowing the cuffs to be put back on.

Sean watched Lee get re-cuffed and escorted out of the room then glanced at the clock on the wall. With noon approaching, he hoped Tasha King would be calling soon with a fingerprint match. In the meantime, he needed to see if one of the laptops matched Monique Butler's missing one.

No point in waiting around for a phone call. Might as well go to the source.

Georgia Bureau of Investigation Headquarters
Panthersville Road
Southeast of Atlanta
12:30 p.m.

As Sean put his car into park, his cell began to ring. "Detective Sparks."

"Sean, it's Tasha King."

"Hey, Tasha. I'm outside your office."

"Okay, so I'll wait until you're *inside* to give you the results."

He laughed. "Fair enough."

He hung up and made a beeline for the lab. Tasha was waiting for him when he entered.

"I'm here."

"Indeed, and I wish I had better news for you."

Sean's smiled dissolved. "Now, Tasha. I can only take so much disappointment on one case from your lab."

She pouted. "Sorry, but I only calls 'em as I sees 'em."

Sean sucked in a long breath. "Okay, let me have it."

"First, the print—it was not a match to Terrance Lee. Second, while I can't rule out the bat as your murder weapon, we didn't find any blood on it."

"Strike one and strike two. What about the laptops?"

"Of course, they did have Lee's prints on them, but I haven't identified who the computers belong to yet."

"Where are they?"

"The laptops?"

"Yeah."

"Over here."

Sean trailed behind her across the lab floor. At a work desk, she pointed out three different computers, each sitting in a plastic bag. Sean recognized the Surface model right away, and his hopes surged. He put on gloves, removed it from the bag, and hit the power button. Nothing.

He took out his phone. "I want to photograph this one and show the pic to Miss Butler. Maybe she can ID it as hers."

"Sounds good."

A few minutes later, he had shots of the front and back, including the serial number. "I guess that's it for now. Thanks for the quick results, Tasha."

"Always glad to be of service."

"I'll let you know what Monique Butler says."

He headed back to his car. With prints and the bat not providing a connection, if the laptop didn't belong to Butler, then confirming Terrance Lee's alibi might just become a formality. A disappointing end to a hopeful lead.

Seems all too common these days.

Atlanta Police Headquarters
Homicide Division
226 Peachtree Street SW
Downtown Atlanta
2:30 p.m.

Sean had made repeated attempts to get a hold of Monique Butler, but her phone was going straight to voicemail. Finally, he dialed Felicity Pope.

"Hello?"

"Mrs. Pope?"

"Yes?"

"This is Detective Sparks."

"Oh, hello, Detective."

"How are you doing?"

"I'm making it, I guess." She sighed. "Despite my issues with Rodney, I never wished him ill."

"I understand. Is Miss Butler there with you?"

"Monique? No."

"I've been trying to reach her. Do you know where she is?"

"Yes. She had some things to take care of at home. She drove back to Savannah."

"I see." Sean didn't like surprises. "Will she be returning to Atlanta?"

"Yes. She planned on driving back here in the morning. She worries about me being alone."

"If you speak with her, would you ask her to call me?"

"I'll be sure to."

"Thanks. Goodbye, Mrs. Pope."

"Goodbye."

He hung up, still irked by Butler's disappearing act. For what seemed the tenth time in the past few days, he chastised himself for not nailing down the details. He should have told her to advise him if she left town.

An uncomfortable sensation prickled the back of his neck.

Was it doubt? Am I starting to question my own abilities?

He shook off the feeling and turned his attention to the pile of papers on his desk. Felicity Pope's and Monique Butler's financial documents had come in. Though most of the suspicion on them had been removed, he needed to complete his due diligence on the pair.

The long, tedious work was mind-numbing but essential.

Welcome to the big time, Sean, old-boy!

****

Four hours and one fast-food dinner later, Sean was working his way through the last of Monique Butler's credit card accounts. So far, he'd come up with what he'd expected—zip.

No money transfers, no large deposits, no suspicious purchases, and no new life insurance policies. Nothing that would lead him in a new direction or cast suspicion on the two people closest to the victim.

He let out a long sigh.

"Having fun, rookie?"

Sean didn't need to look up to know who was standing over him. "Hey, Lance."

Henderson smiled widely, his perfect front teeth nearly illuminating the room as much as the shine off the top of his bald head. "About the only thing more fun than financials is phone records."

Sean groaned. "Already had the pleasure of doing those."

"Find anything?"

"Nah. This case is going nowhere fast."

Henderson's smile disappeared, replaced by a sincere gaze as he locked eyes with Sean. "How long you been working this now? Four days?"

"Five."

"Look, I know it's drummed into your head that the first forty-eight hours are critical, and they are, but a huge number of cases take days, weeks, even months, to figure out. Don't get down on yourself. Remember—keep poking the bear."

That was another one of Henderson's favorite sayings. When cases started to look like they might go cold, he would say, *"Keep poking the sleeping bear. Eventually, he'll get mad and show you his teeth."*

"I remember." Sean managed a weak smile. "Thanks."

Henderson cocked his head to one side. "Did I ever tell you the story about the last detective I trained who *didn't* make it in homicide?"

"No, I guess not."

"That's because it hasn't happened. I don't sign off on investigators unless they can cut it."

Sean shrugged. "I hope I'm not the first."

"You don't understand." Henderson leaned over and got directly in Sean's face. "You're not going to be the first because you're good."

Sean looked into his mentor's eyes for a long moment. "Thanks."

Henderson stood up, and his smile returned. "Now get back to work. I don't want Mitchell accusing me of wasting your time."

Sean gave him a mock salute. "Aye, Aye, Captain."

Henderson wandered off as Sean worked the last few pages of Butler's Mastercard. Near the bottom, he came across the bill for the hotel room. He paused and stared.

Didn't I already see the hotel charge?

He checked the date. Monday, December 18—the day after the murder. That matched the date Felicity and Monique needed to start staying in a hotel following the murder.

He sifted through the previous pages of the card statement until he found it. Another charge for a room in the same hotel, only this one was three days *before* the murder. Sean's radar was pinging now. Butler never mentioned staying at a hotel, and her suitcase had been in the guest bedroom upstairs.

Sean considered calling Monique and asking her about the earlier charge, but he figured he'd just get her voicemail again. He could call Felicity, but something inside said not to. Instead, he scooped up the Mastercard statement and went to his car.

Comfort Inn
795 Pollard Blvd SW
South Atlanta
6:45 p.m.

Sean arrived at the six-story hotel built in the familiar beige concrete to find the parking lot packed; not surprising, considering Christmas day was just around the corner. Lots of tourists liked to come to the city and attend the numerous holiday events.

Inside, every orange and teal lobby chair was filled, and the entrance foyer was a beehive of activity. He crossed the entranceway of ceramic tile laid to look like wood planks and waited for the harried clerk to have a spare moment.

The man glanced at Sean. "Welcome to Comfort Inn. I'll be with you in a moment."

"No hurry."

After handing over keys to a room and answering a phone call, the Hispanic clerk turned to Sean. "Thank you for your patience. Do you have a reservation?"

"No." Sean showed his badge. "I'm Detective Sparks with Atlanta PD. Is the manager here?"

"I'm the night manager—Eddie Marcos."

"Great. Busy night, huh?"

"Thanksgiving, Christmas, and New Years are always nuts. What can I help you with?"

Sean extracted a page of Butler's Mastercard statement from a folder he carried and handed it to Marcos. "Can you look up this reservation for me?"

Marcos studied it then tapped some keys on his computer. He ran a finger across the screen. "Here it is. The room was rented for three nights by a Monique Butler. She paid for it with the card on this statement."

"Does it list the occupants?"

"No. We have her license on file because she rented the room, but no other names."

"What kind of room was it?"

"A single king bed."

Sean retrieved the statement sheet. "Do you have cameras in the hotel's hallways?"

"Sure. Two on every floor, pointing in opposite directions from the elevator."

An idea percolated up in Sean's head. "What room was given to Miss Butler?"

"205."

"Eddie—is that right?"

"Yes."

"Eddie, can you show me the camera footage on that floor from the days around the reservation?"

"Sure, if I don't get swamped again. You'll have to come into the back with me, though."

Sean nodded and followed the manager into a small office behind the front desk. Eddie sat in a chair, looked at the dates on the statement, then started cycling through the footage. The hotel appeared to have at least twenty cameras, maybe more.

After several minutes, Eddie picked a single shot and filled the screen with it. "This looks down on the north end of the second floor. The room in question is the third door on the right—number 205."

A bell on the front desk rang.

The manager pushed back his chair. "I've chosen to start it just moments after the check-in time listed on the reservation."

"Perfect."

Marcos stood. "Just push the arrow keys to make it go forward or backward. You can stop it with this button. I'll be back in a moment."

"No problem. Thanks."

Sean took the manager's seat at the desk and pushed the play button. The video began to roll, but since there wasn't any activity, it continued to look like a still shot. Nearly ten full minutes passed before a single male carrying a duffle bag walked into frame. The man stopped at 205, swiped the key card, glanced back toward the elevator, then disappeared into the room.

Sean's heart pounded in his ears as he backed up the video to the moment when the man swiped his key card. Sean hit play, and a half second later, he froze the shot. Looking back at the camera was a young man, or more accurately, a teenager. The individual appeared to be no older than eighteen or nineteen, slight in build, with short hair and an ordinary face.

Marcos returned from the front desk. "How's it going?"

Sean pointed at the frozen screen. "Eddie, do you remember him?"

The manager nodded. "I think so. Although, I can't say I talked to him."

"How about anything unusual about him, like a piece of clothing or a hat?"

Marcos shook his head. "Not that I remember."

"Did you see him *with* anyone?"

"No, I don't think so. But as you've seen, it gets pretty crazy around here."

"Sure. Can you print that for me?"

"Yes," Marcos reached around Sean and punched two buttons simultaneously. "It will print out by the desk."

"Good, And I'll need a copy of this camera's video for the entire three days the room was rented by this individual."

"Okay."

The phone rang again.

Eddie glanced over his shoulder toward the front desk and sighed. "But I'll have to send that over to you."

"That's fine." Sean handed him a business card.

Eddie went out to the front desk area, and Sean followed. Eddie greeted the woman at the desk then reached over and picked up the printed image of the mystery man. He handed it to Sean.

"Thanks, Eddie. I imagine the room has been rented out several times since then?"

Eddie went to his computer screen. "Yes, three times."

"Is it rented now?"

"Yes."

"Can you tell me when the current occupant leaves?"

Marcos smiled at the woman waiting. "I'm sorry, ma'am. I'll just be a moment longer."

He tapped on the keyboard. "They check out in the morning."

The odds of finding evidence in the room were remote, but Sean had to have it searched anyway. "I'll need you to seal the room. Don't let anyone else inside—especially the cleaning crew. I'll have a forensic team over here by noon tomorrow."

Marcos shrugged. "Okay, but I'll have to notify the hotel manager."

"That's fine. You said that room has a king bed only?"

"Correct."

"I'll let you get back to work. Thanks again."

"You're welcome."

Marcos turned to the now impatient woman at the desk while Sean headed back out to his car. Within the quiet of his vehicle, he stared at the image on the photo.

A single bed in the room suggested the man was the only person staying there, which meant Monique Butler rented it specifically for him. But why?

Next on Sean's agenda—identify the man in the picture. But how?

Should he confront Monique Butler? Maybe check with Felicity Pope? Either way, Butler would be tipped off that he had the photo, which might not be the best avenue to take.

His phone rang, startling him and interrupting his train of thought.

He looked at the number. *Monique Butler. Speak of the devil...*

Not ready to reveal what he'd learned, he answered with his guard up. "Detective Sparks."

"Detective, this is Monique Butler. I got your messages."

"Yes, thank you for calling back. We recovered a laptop that could be yours, and I wanted to show the photos to you."

An obvious hesitation. "That's great. I'm in Savannah, though."

"Your mother had mentioned that. Will you be returning tomorrow as she said?"

"Yes. I worry about her, you know."

"Of course."

"I'm leaving first thing in the morning."

"Perhaps you could stop by my office on the way."

"I'd be glad to. I think I may have the laptop's serial number here at the house, so I'll see if I can find it and bring it with me."

"Excellent. See you around noon tomorrow?"

"Okay. Goodbye."

"Bye."

The line went dead. Sean had until noon the next day to decide how he would use the hotel information when he talked with Butler.

Whatever I decide, it should turn out to be a very interesting conversation.

ATLANTA HOMICIDE

<u>Saturday, December 23</u>

Home of Detective Sean Sparks
Camden Vantage Apartments
Sweet Auburn Neighborhood
East of Downtown Atlanta
8:15 a.m.

Mariah sat across from Sean at the small kitchen table and toyed with her eggs. "Tomorrow's Christmas Eve."

Sean raised an eyebrow. "It is, isn't it?"

The surprise in his voice was genuine. Even though he was constantly bombarded with the holiday everywhere he went, his mind had remained consumed with the case.

She looked at him with wide eyes. "You can't forget Christmas!"

He grinned at her. "Of course not. I'm just not doing a great job keeping track of what day it is."

She eyed him suspiciously. "You claimed to have my present figured out. I hope you haven't forgotten."

Her gift was one thing that hadn't been put aside—it was safely tucked away where she couldn't find it. "I haven't forgotten."

"Will you be able to come over to Mom and Dad's tomorrow night?"

He shrugged. "I really don't know. Things are in flux right now, so I don't want to make promises."

She pouted, which only made her cuter than she already was. He laid his hand on top of hers.

"I promise to do my best."

The edge of her lips curled upward. "That's good enough for me."

"Anyway, as much as I appreciate the cooked breakfast"—he stood—"I need to take off."

"Okay, I'll clean up a little before I head out."

"You're the best." He kissed her cheek. "Love you."

"Love you more."

He kissed her again. "Not possible."

Office of Lieutenant Shannon Mitchell
Atlanta Police Headquarters
Homicide Division
226 Peachtree Street SW
Downtown Atlanta
10:45 a.m.

Sean waited, letting his boss consider his latest update. The surveillance photo from Comfort Inn sat on the lieutenant's desk in front of her.

She fingered the edge of picture. "He's young."

Sean nodded. "My first impression was nineteen or twenty."

"And the hotel had no information on who he was?"

"No. Apparently, Monique Butler gave him the key without registering him as the guest."

Mitchell squinted at the photo, as if trying to see something that was hiding just below the surface. "And the video didn't show anyone with him?"

He shook his head. "I went through all the footage this morning. Our mystery guy was the only one going in and out of the room."

"I gather you had just about cleared Butler until this came up, is that right?"

He nodded. "I have nothing to suggest she was involved, and if there's a reasonable explanation for her paying the bill on this room, then I will officially be done with her."

"I admit, this is troubling, but by itself, it's no indication of her being involved with her stepfather's death." She pursed her lips. "What's your strategy?"

"That's where I was hoping for some guidance. I'm not sure whether to be confrontational with Butler, go to her mother first and pretend curiosity, or keep it to myself until a moment that seems more fitting than the interview."

"You have a meeting with Miss Butler when?"

"Supposed to be noon. She's coming in from Savannah."

Mitchell glanced down at the clock on her desk—a crystal plaque on a stand with a watch face embedded, which had been awarded to her several years ago for saving the life of a fellow officer.

"Here's what I suggest. Take her into Interview 1 and show her the photo. Judge whether to press her forcefully or not by her reaction. Then choose your follow up questions at that time. I'll be in the observation suite where I can observe her body language. After the interview, we'll compare notes."

143

Sean liked it. His preference had been to spring the photo on Butler, but he'd remained unsure of the decision, even after pondering it all night.

"Works for me."

"Okay," She slid the photo back to him. "Let me know when she gets here."

"Yes, ma'am."

Sean stepped out of the office as his desk phone rang. He reached over and grabbed it.

"Homicide—Detective Sparks speaking."

"Yes, Detective, this is Sergeant Perkins at the front desk. I have a Miss Butler here to see you."

Sean glanced at his watch. She was nearly an hour early.

"Very good. Have her taken to Interview Room 1, please."

"Yes, sir."

Sean turned around and went back to the lieutenant's office.

"She's here."

Mitchell looked up. "Already?"

He shrugged. "Anxious to make a good impression, maybe?"

She smirked. "More likely no traffic."

He smiled. "She's on her way to Room 1."

Mitchell pushed back from her desk and stood. "Let's go."

Interview Room 1
Atlanta Police Headquarters
Homicide Division
226 Peachtree Street SW
Downtown Atlanta
11:20 a.m.

Sean had waited for Lieutenant Mitchell to get situated then tapped on the door to announce his presence, before walking into the small room.

He carried a single sheet of paper and four photos. "Good morning, Miss Butler. Thank you for coming in."

"Of course, and please call me Monique."

"Very well." He laid the paper and photos face down on the table. "Would you like anything to drink?"

"No, thank you. I was hoping we could do this quickly. I want to get over to my mother's as soon as possible."

An oversized purse sat on the floor next to her and she had folded a long coat over the back of her chair.

Sean settled into the seat across from her. "I don't imagine it will take long to go over the couple things I need." He flipped over two of the photos. "These are of the front and back of a Surface 3 we confiscated during an arrest."

"Oh," She glanced at the pictures then reached down and pulled a piece of paper out of her purse. "I found the serial number for my laptop."

"Good." Sean accepted the note. "I have the serial number of the confiscated unit right here."

He flipped over the third photo and compared the numbers. "That's disappointing." They don't match.

She frowned. "It's not mine?"

"I'm afraid not."

"Oh, that's too bad."

Was it his imagination, or did she seem relieved?

He took the three face-up photos and moved them aside in a separate pile. Monique's gaze moved to the remaining hidden items. Sean fidgeted with the top sheet, testing the woman's patience. Her eyes were locked on the paper.

"So…" He kept his tone casual. "In doing my regular review of bank records and such, I found something I couldn't recall us talking about."

Her eyes flicked up to meet his stare then back to the paper. "Oh?"

"Specifically, on your Mastercard statement."

"My Mastercard?" Her face muscles tightened. "Why would you be interested in that?"

He shrugged. "Just normal *T* crossing and *I* dotting."

"I see. What could possibly have troubled you on my card?"

"It's a charge to the Comfort Inn."

"The Comfort Inn?" She appeared confused. "That's where Mom and I stayed after my stepfather's death."

"Yes." Sean flipped the page over. "But this was for a room three days prior to your stay there."

Monique stiffened and stared at him. Then, out of the blue, she smiled. "Oh, that! You're absolutely right—I did forget to mention him."

It was Sean's turn to be surprised. "Forget to mention who?"

146

"The young man I ran into on my way to visit mom."

"Ran into where?"

"The Exxon station in Morrow."

Sean placed Morrow in his mind. The small town was south of the city and actually more of an Atlanta suburb than its own entity. He flipped the last photo over. "Is this him?"

Butler grinned and tapped the picture. "Yeah, that's Jack."

"Jack? Do you know his last name?"

"No. He was a nice boy and in a tough spot, so I helped him out."

Sean resisted the urge to look back at the observation room, but he could guess what Mitchell's thoughts were. Probably the same as his—*is she for real?* He half expected his lieutenant to come barging into the room and scoff at Butler.

He refocused. "Please tell me about him, Monique."

She shrugged. "Not much to tell, really. I stopped for coffee and to use the bathroom in Morrow, and he was sitting outside. When I went in to pay, he asked me if I was going to Atlanta. I said I was, and he asked if I would mind giving him a ride."

Sean tipped his head to one side. "Do you regularly give rides to strangers?"

She chuckled. "No, certainly not, but he seemed harmless, and I felt sorry for him."

"Why?"

"He said he'd been traveling with friends from Florida, and they'd dumped him. He wanted me to take him to the Atlanta Mission, where he hoped they could help him get on his feet."

"How did you end up paying for his hotel room?"

147

"Like I said, I felt bad for him, and those shelters are no place for a kid. While we were driving into the city, he said he wanted to start his life over in Atlanta. I offered to put him up for a few days until he got settled."

"Do you know where he is now?"

She shook her head slowly. "Not a clue. Like I said, I just wanted to help him out."

Her demeanor was so calm, Sean found himself accepting the story. She wouldn't be the first soft-hearted person to help out a young stranger. Still, what if Jack had seen an opportunity and decided to take advantage of the situation?

"Did you mention why you were coming to Atlanta? You know, talk about where *you* were going and such?"

She furrowed her brow. "I suppose. I'm not sure. Why?"

"Is it possible he learned where your mother lived and decided to rob the place?"

Her eyes widened. "No…no…I can't imagine that. He was too nice."

"You said the gas station was in Morrow?"

"Yes, the Exxon just off I-75." She glanced at her watch. "Detective, if that's all…I really need to go."

Sean gathered his papers but remained seated. "I understand. That'll do for now."

She stood and scooped up her purse. "Very well."

"Please give your mother my best."

"I will. Good day."

She left, and moments later, Mitchell came in and leaned against the wall. "That was interesting."

He grimaced. "You can say that again. You think she's telling the truth?"

She turned up her palms. "Honestly, I'm not sure. At first, the story seemed preposterous, but…"

"Yeah, me, too. However, she seemed comfortable explaining it, so I can't be sure."

Mitchell crossed her arms. "What do you plan to do next?"

"I guess I'll go out to the gas station and show the picture around. Maybe someone else remembers the man, or maybe the station has him on video."

She nodded. "Exactly what I would do."

He pushed himself up out of the small chair. "Thanks for observing."

She smiled. "Anytime."

Exxon Station
6629 Jonesboro Road
Morrow, Georgia
South of Atlanta
12:45 p.m.

Just fifteen miles outside Atlanta, Sean found the Morrow Exxon easily. He pulled up in front of the station and got out, pulling his jacket tight around him. The wind was starting to feel like a white Christmas might be a reality—it carried a nasty bite.

The station was busy, but he was able to get the clerk's attention long enough to ask where the manager's office was.

"Back in the corner, past the coolers."

149

He nodded and followed the directions to the rear of the store. The office door sat slightly ajar, and Sean could see an African-American woman in her thirties sitting at the tiny desk. He tapped on the frame.

She looked up. "Come in."

He pushed the door open. "Are you the manager?"

"I am. Can I help you?"

Sean showed her his badge. "I'm Detective Sparks with Atlanta PD."

"Leticia Hunter." Concern marred her otherwise pretty face. "Is there a problem?"

"No. I just need some information."

"What sort of information?"

Sean pulled a copy of the hotel photo out of his folder and handed it to her. "Do you recognize this man?"

She stared at it briefly. "I don't think so. Why?"

"He was here last week. I'm hoping you can find him on your video."

She handed it back. "What day was that?"

"A week ago Friday."

She glanced up at a calendar on the wall. "That would be the fifteenth."

"Right."

"Well, I have good news and bad news for you."

Sean smiled. "Okay, how about the good news first."

"Our cameras overwrite every thirty days, so I will have video that day."

Sean's hopes climbed. "And the bad?"

"The pump cameras were out of service last week. We just got them back on line two days ago."

"But the inside cameras were operational?"

"That's right."

"Well, I'm a glass-half-full kind a guy, so I'll take what I can get."

"Do you know what time he was here?"

Sean had the Mastercard statement for the transaction. "Between ten and eleven that morning should cover it."

Hunter rotated in her seat and began typing on a keyboard. The monitor to her right came to life and showed four camera angles—behind the register, in front of the register, the doors, and the back of the store. Hunter spun a knob and raced through a bunch of video before slowing to a stop.

"This is five past ten that morning."

The video crept forward at half-speed, and it didn't take long before Monique Butler came through the door. Sean's adrenaline surged. "That's her."

"Her?" Hunter gave him a sideways glance. "We're not looking for the man in the photo?"

Sean nodded. "We are, but he was supposedly with that woman."

Next through the door was the young man on the picture. He stopped next to Butler, and they interacted for several moments until Monique paid. Then they walked out the door together.

Sean watched them disappear from camera view in the direction of the parking lot. "No shots of the pumps, right?"

"Afraid not."

"Okay. Can you play it again?"

Hunter backed it up and replayed the video. "They seem friendly enough."

They do, don't they? "I'd like to get a copy of that."

151

"I'll have to send the request through corporate."

Sean handed her a business card. "That's fine. Send it to this address, please."

"Okay. Anything else?"

"No. Thanks for your help."

He headed back out to his car.

Sitting in front of the station, he played the video back in his mind. Something just didn't feel right. The video matched Butler's story, but...

He got an idea. Taking out the Mastercard statement, he examined it, then put the car in drive. He merged onto the interstate, going south, away from Atlanta.

Marathon Gas Station
Georgia Highway 121
Metter, Georgia
200 Miles Southeast of Atlanta
4:00 p.m.

Sean drove for two and a half hours before pulling off at the Marathon gas station in the town of Metter, a bustling community of roughly five thousand just an hour outside Savannah. He parked and got out, immediately noticing the milder temperature. The combination of being two hundred miles farther south and considerably closer to the ocean meant the cold hadn't penetrated this far.

Sean stretched his arms and back before stripping off his coat and tossing it into the car.

152

As he entered, the lone clerk smiled. "Welcome to Marathon."

"Thanks. Manager here?"

"Assistant manager is in the office."

"Where's that?"

"Go down the little hallway behind me, past the bathrooms, and you'll see the door."

"Thanks."

Sean had consumed multiple cups of coffee on his drive, so he paused to use the facilities before going to the office.

A man in his late fifties with thinning hair and a gray goatee looked up from his desk. "Can I help you?"

Sean had his badge out. "Detective Sparks—Atlanta police department."

"Walt Cooper." They shook. "Atlanta? You're a long way from home."

Sean smiled wearily. "Don't I know it."

"What do you need?"

"I'm hoping you have security video from a week ago Friday—the fifteenth."

"Sure. We keep ours on a sixty day loop."

"I'm interested in a woman who bought gas here that day between seven-thirty and eight in the morning. I have a credit card statement for the transaction."

"Okay. Let's see what we have." Cooper stood and pointed down the hall. "Video screens are behind the counter."

Sean stepped aside. "Lead the way."

They walked past the bathrooms and up onto an elevated area that contained the cigarette racks, registers, and a counter with a set of monitors showing the camera views. Cooper immediately started typing on the console then turned to Sean.

"Let me see the card statement."

Sean handed it to him. "It's near the bottom."

Cooper studied it then handed it back. "It says the purchase was made on pump three." He rotated another knob and pushed a button, changing the picture on the monitor from a four-shot view to a single-shot. "Here we go. Tell me when you see the car."

Sean watched the video move forward. A red pick-up finished gassing up then drove away. Moments later, a blue Honda pulled up at the pump.

Sean nodded. "That's her."

Several seconds passed, then the passenger door opened. Sean realized he was holding his breath. A leg swung out of that side of the car, then a young man stepped out, turning toward the camera.

"*Stop!*"

The picture froze.

The silence behind him caused Sean to turn his head. The clerk and two customers were motionless, staring at him.

He grinned. "I'm sorry. I was talking to him."

The clerk smiled and returned to checking out the customers.

Cooper laughed. "I think you scared them."

Sean rubbed his chin. "Yeah, sorry about that. Can you print the photo for me?"

"Sure."

A printer off to Sean's right came to life. He touched Cooper's shoulder. "Let it roll some more."

The video started forward again. The male opened the gas tank and started filling the car. The other door opened, and Monique Butler stepped out. She walked toward the camera, heading inside the store.

"Stop it there, please."

Cooper did. "Another printed copy?"

"Please."

Sean stared at the screen. *You have some explaining to do, Miss Butler. You didn't pick up Jack in Morrow. And Jack—if that's his name—is likely no stranger to you.*

Cooper went to the printer and returned with the two photos. Sean traded a business card for them. "Thanks. Send a copy of the video to that address."

"Be glad to."

"Mind if I grab a coffee before heading out."

Cooper smiled. "For one of Atlanta's finest—make it a coffee *and* a donut!"

Sean laughed, his spirits lifted by his new find. "Good deal!"

Ten minutes later, he was on his way back to Atlanta.

Sean called Felicity Pope.

"Hello?"

"Mrs. Pope, it's Detective Sparks."

"Oh, hello."

"I wondered if you were going to be home this evening?"

"As of now, I don't have plans to go anywhere."

"Then would it be okay if I came by?"

"Of course."

"Is your daughter also there?"

"No. She's out with Bill. He came in off the road, and they met downtown. Do you need to speak with her?"

Sean considered the question. Perhaps showing the photo to Felicity, without Monique hovering around, would result in something new.

"No, it's not important right now. I'll come by and see you, though."

"Very well. When?"

"I'm on the road." Sean glanced at the clock on his dash. "So I would guess between eight and eight-thirty.'

"That'll be fine. See you then."

Home of Rodney and Felicity Pope
2905 Renfro Drive NW
Collier Heights Neighborhood
West Atlanta
8:15 p.m.

Right on time, he climbed out of the car at the Pope residence.

He'd spent over eight hours in the car, and his body was complaining about it, so he took a moment to stretch his stiff muscles then headed up to the front door. With the folder of photos in hand, he rang the bell.

A smiling and seemingly more at ease Felicity Pope opened the door. Her hair was tied back in a ponytail, and she wore blue jogging pants and a long-sleeved white shirt.

"Come in, Detective."

156

"Thank you."

"Would you like something to drink? I'm having a glass of wine, myself."

He smiled. "I better not."

"Of course."

The fact that the front hall had been scrubbed of the blood was not surprising, but the Christmas tree in the corner of the living room seemed to be a quick adjustment. She apparently caught his gaze.

"Monique insisted on putting up the tree. She said it would serve as a distraction."

Sean nodded. "May I sit?"

"Please do."

He lowered himself onto the couch. "Is your daughter due back soon?"

"No." Felicity sat in the chair opposite him and took a sip of her wine. "Bill got tickets for the two of them to ride the Skyview. After dinner, they're staying in a hotel downtown"

The Skyview was a twenty-story-high Ferris wheel on Centennial Plaza and would no doubt be a great place to see the Christmas lights of downtown. "That should be a real treat."

She smiled. "I told her I was fine with a night to myself."

"I'm sorry to barge in then. It won't take long."

She dismissed his concern with a wave. "It's no problem. In fact, the quiet was starting to get to me, but I wanted Monique to focus on herself for one night."

He smiled. "She is protective."

"To her own detriment, I fear. I purposely didn't tell her you had called because I know she would have come home."

157

"You're probably right." He opened the folder. "I have a photo I'd like to show you. This individual has surfaced in some video I've been going over, and I'm unable to identify him."

After setting her wine down, she accepted the picture he held out.

A warm smile lit up her face. "Oh, that's Kenny."

Sean's eyebrows spiked upward. "Kenny?"

She handed the photo back. "My grandson."

He wasn't sure he'd heard right. "Did you say your *grandson?*"

"Yes, though it's not a very good picture of him."

Sean resisted the urge to collapse backward against the couch, even though a tsunami of realization was surging over him. "What is Kenny's last name?"

"Butler. He's Monique's son."

Whether it was exhaustion or something else, Sean's mind spun so fast, his stomach churned as if he might vomit. His thoughts raced, overloading his brain with questions.

How did I not know Monique Butler had a son?
Hadn't she said she'd never been married?
Was there some question I forgot to ask?
Why didn't I inquire about children?

He looked around the room. "I don't see any photos of your grandson."

She sighed. "Rodney and Kenny didn't see eye to eye, so I preferred not to upset Rodney by putting photos on display. I made up for it by having plenty on my phone and in my albums."

John C. Dalglish

Sean was doing his best to catch up with the runaway train that was his thoughts. "What was the issue between them?"

"Honestly, I'm not sure. They just never got along. Rodney preferred not to talk about it, and I never asked Kenny."

He had his pad out now. "Miss Butler and Kenny's father were never married?"

"No, they were very young. Monique raised Kenny until he was fourteen, but he became a handful, so Kenny's father agreed to take him in."

"What is his father's name?"

"Isaac Ortega."

"And where does Mr. Ortega live?"

"Metter—about an hour north of Savannah."

That was the first piece of information that didn't come as a total surprise. Monique probably stopped at the Marathon station in Metter after picking up Kenny from his father's.

But could a young man of Kenny's slight build inflict the damage that killed Rodney Pope?

Sean wondered about Isaac Ortega. Maybe his stature would fit the crime better.

"Do you have any photos of Mr. Ortega?"

She shook her head. "No, we were never that close. Monique and Isaac only dated for a few months before the pregnancy happened. You know how those things are."

"What is the relationship between your daughter and Mr. Ortega these days?"

"As far as I know, they only communicate about Kenny. Monique still picks him up for visits on a regular basis." She

159

tipped her head to one side. "Why all the focus on Kenny? He couldn't hurt a fly."

"Just tying up loose ends is all." Sean put away his notepad and closed the folder. Suddenly very anxious to get to the precinct, he stood. "Thanks for your time, Mrs. Pope."

"Of course. You sure you won't have that glass of wine now?"

"Nope. Unfortunately, I'm still on the clock. Goodnight."

He trotted through the cold evening air and jumped into the car. His head now throbbed with the amount of information Felicity Pope had delivered, but his next task was clear. Find out as much as he could about Kenny Butler and Isaac Ortega.

Atlanta Police Headquarters
Homicide Division
226 Peachtree Street SW
Downtown Atlanta
10:15 p.m.

On the drive down to the precinct, Sean realized that as a juvenile, even if Kenny had been in trouble, his prints might not be in AFIS. The father, Isaac Ortega, was a different story. If Ortega was involved, then he couldn't have a record, or the print on the casino mug would have gotten a hit.

Once he reached his desk, he typed in the name Isaac Ortega, and the man's driver's license popped up. Though the photo only showed from the neck up, Ortega's information listed him as a five-foot-eleven and a hundred and ninety pounds, plenty big enough to do damage with a baseball bat. His thick hair was black, as was his bushy moustache.

He had no criminal record, so nothing to indicate he could be violent. The only things that came up were a couple citations for speeding—and being in a hurry does not a murderer make. Sean didn't have anything to indicate Ortega was involved in Rodney Pope's death, and the file certainly didn't suggest otherwise.

Still, the lack of a criminal record left open the possibility of Ortega being a match to the thumb print on the casino mug. Of greater importance was the fact that Kenny was on camera in Atlanta around the time of the murder, which, so far, could not be said about Ortega.

He needed to talk with both of them, but Kenny Butler would be first, which meant finding him.

"How's it going?"

Sean turned to find Lieutenant Mitchell standing behind him. "Lieutenant? You're here late."

"The same could be said for you."

"Yes, ma'am."

"Learn anything new today?"

He rolled his eyes. "You wouldn't believe."

"Try me."

"You know the photo I showed you this morning?"

"The young man at the hotel?"

"Yeah. Well, I got an ID on him. His name is Kenny Butler."

Mitchell's eyes flared. "As in *Monique* Butler?"

"One in the same. Kenny Butler is Monique's son and Mrs. Pope's grandson."

"No kidding? That must have come as a surprise."

"At first, I thought my ears were playing tricks on me."

"I bet. What about the father? Get a line on him?"

"Yes." He tapped the computer screen. "His name is Isaac Ortega, age forty-three. A couple speeding tickets is all we have on him. Not sure why he would be involved."

"You should talk with both anyway."

"Absolutely, but particularly the grandson, since he was in town before the murder."

"Where does he live?"

"Metter."

She nodded. "I know where that is. Call Metter police and see if they can arrange an interview with Kenny Butler."

"I'll do it."

"Meanwhile, while they hunt him down, you get some sleep. I'm guessing you haven't gotten much rest in the last few days."

Sean gave her a sheepish grin. "I got a little sleep yesterday evening."

"Get a little more before you make the drive back down to Metter—got it?"

"Yes, ma'am."

"Good."

She headed for the elevator while Sean looked up the number for the Metter police and dialed it.

"Metter police department."

"Yes, this is Detective Sparks with the Atlanta PD. I'd like to speak to your duty sergeant."

"You got him—Sergeant Xavier."

162

"Good evening, Sergeant. I need your department's help with something."

"Be glad to if we can. What you need?"

"I'm trying to locate a Kenny Butler, age nineteen. He's supposed to live with his father, Isaac Ortega, at 442 South Rountree."

"I'm familiar with the street. It's only a mile and half from here."

"I need to speak with Butler in reference to a murder case I'm working. Do you think you could go by the house and see if he's there?"

"Sure. Do you want us to pick him up?"

"No, not unless he gives you a problem. See if he'll agree to an interview at your station in the morning."

"We can do that."

"If he asks what it's about, say his grandfather's death."

"I'll pass that on to the officer. Is there concern with either party at the home being armed?"

"Not to my knowledge, but you know the drill…"

"We'll be cautious."

"Appreciate it." Sean gave his cellphone number to the sergeant. "Just let me know what he says. If he agrees, I'll drive down first thing."

"You got it."

Sean hung up. *Time to get some shut-eye—Lieutenant's orders.*

Home of Detective Sean Sparks
Camden Vantage Apartments
Sweet Auburn Neighborhood
East of Downtown Atlanta
11:30 p.m.

Sean was just settling into bed when his phone rang.
"Sparks."

"Detective, this is Sergeant Xavier with Metter PD."

"Hey. Any news?"

"Yes. We made contact with Mr. Ortega."

"Was Butler home?"

"He was, but he had already gone to sleep. Ortega didn't like police coming to his door at that hour, so he refused to wake his son. Our officer asked if he would bring his son down to the station in the morning for an interview."

"How did Ortega react?"

"At first, he was pissed and wanted to know what we wanted with his son. When we explained the request came from Atlanta PD in reference to the boy's grandfather, he changed his tune."

"Did he agree to come down?"

"He did—eight a.m."

Sean glanced at his clock. With drive time, he would get about four hours sleep—better than nothing. "Thanks for your help. I'll be in touch when I get close to town."

"You're welcome. Chief Vincent will be in by then, so you can ask for him."

"Perfect. Goodnight."

Sean hung up, threw his legs up onto the bed, and cut off the light. His mind focused on the anticipated interview in the morning. It just might break open the case. He looked at the clock. How was he to unwind?

Man, I need to think about something else, or I'm never going to get to slee...

ATLANTA HOMICIDE

John C. Dalglish

Sunday, December 24

Christmas Eve

Home of Detective Sean Sparks
Camden Vantage Apartments
Sweet Auburn Neighborhood
East of Downtown Atlanta
4:05 a.m.

Mariah's music of choice for Sean to wake up to was an *Imagine Dragons* song titled *On Top of the World*. At four o'clock in the morning, he didn't feel on top of anything. He groaned and reached over to shut off the music then forced himself out of bed.

The room was chilly, and the cold reminded Sean it was Christmas Eve. Depending on how his interviews with Kenny Butler and Isaac Ortega went, he might have to beg off from the gathering at Mariah's parents', which would surely disappoint her and put a kink in his own plans.

He made his way unsteadily to the bathroom and did his best to put on a fresh face.

Thirty minutes later, he checked himself out in the dining room mirror. All things considered, he'd made himself into something resembling a detective—no small accomplishment. Next stop, Metter.

On the drive down, Sean made two phone calls. Mariah was first.

"Hello?" The sleepiness in her voice told him he'd woken her.

"Good morning."

"Good *early* morning, you mean?"

"Yeah, that's what I meant."

"Where are you?"

"On my way to Metter."

"Metter? Where's that?"

"About an hour outside of Savannah."

"Oh." She yawned. "I'd ask why, but I'm sure it's too long a story for this early."

He laughed. "You're probably right."

"Will you make it for Christmas Eve with my folks?"

"I don't know. The case is moving pretty fast, and I'm not sure what the situation will be by then."

She fell silent.

He sighed. "You're pouting, aren't you?"

She laughed. "Maybe."

"I promise to do my best."

"I know you will. Love you."

"Love you more."

"Not…" She yawned a second time. "Possible."

After hanging up, Sean had gotten an inspiration. He called Chief Vincent.

"This is Vincent."

"Detective Sparks, Atlanta PD."

"Good morning. I was told to expect your call."

"Sergeant Xavier was very helpful last night."

"He's a good man, and we're always glad to help our compatriots in law enforcement." Vincent's gravelly voice oozed departmental pride. "We work with the officers down

168

in Savannah fairly often, but I don't remember the last time Atlanta PD needed something."

Sean laughed. "The world gets smaller all the time, it seems."

"Too true! Too true!"

"Did Mr. Ortega and his son show up?"

"They did. I have them in an interview room."

"I wonder if I could get another favor."

"Shoot."

"I'd like to do a search of the Ortega home *before* the interviews. Perhaps you could have an officer run the father back over to the house for me."

"I'll do it myself. When will you be in town?"

"Ten minutes."

"We'll see you there."

"Thanks."

Home of Isaac Ortega
422 South Rountree Street
Metter, Georgia
8:10 a.m.

Eight minutes later, Sean pulled up at the Ortega home.

Chief Vincent got out of his vehicle and came over to Sean's car. "Good morning again, Detective Sparks."

Sean got out and shook hands with the barrel-chested man, whose shaved head, forceful grip, and penetrating blue eyes reminded Sean of a dock worker he'd once known. "I appreciate the help. Did you tell Mr. Ortega why he's here?"

"No. Just told him you wanted to meet with him. I have a couple officers on the way to help with the search if he allows it."

"Excellent. We'll be looking for anything with blood on it, specifically a baseball bat. Also, a Microsoft laptop."

"Got it."

Sean looked toward the house. The brick ranch with a tan roof and beige shutters appeared to be well kept from the outside. This far south, the grass still got cut occasionally, despite the time of year, and the lawn was neatly trimmed.

Isaac Ortega stood on the small covered front porch, his back against the wall and his arms crossed in front of his chest. He wore the blue shirt and pants of a U.S. Postal employee. When Sean stepped up on the porch, Ortega stared warily at him, the man's dark moustache twitching.

Sean extended his hand. "Mr. Ortega, I'm Detective Sparks with the Atlanta police department."

Ortega reluctantly unfolded his arms and shook. "Isaac Ortega."

"Sir, as I believe you were told, I'm investigating the murder of Kenny's step-grandfather, Rodney Pope."

Ortega nodded, his arms returning to across his chest. "I'm not sure what we could help you with."

"It's standard practice to interview everyone in the deceased person's family circle. Kenny certainly is part of that." Sean looked at the front door. "Would it be okay if we went inside?"

Ortega shrugged then unlocked the door. He led the way in, and Sean followed, as did Vincent.

Sean let his eyes adjust then smiled. "Okay if we take a look around?"

The man's scowl clearly indicated it was *not* okay, but apparently, he preferred not to make an issue out of Sean's request. "I guess."

Sean turned to Vincent, who nodded and went outside. The home was tidy for a single man and a teenage boy. Sean scanned the living room, taking note of the photos on the wall. Plenty of Kenny and even one of Kenny and his grandmother, but no sign of Monique. Hardly a surprise.

Vincent returned with two officers in tow. They spread out and began to search.

Sean gestured toward the kitchen. "Mind if you and I sit at the table and chat?"

Ortega lumbered toward the table without saying a word. Sean followed and sat opposite him.

Once his notepad was out, he met the man's stare. "Mr. Ortega, where was Kenny last Sunday night?"

"With Monique, visiting his grandmother."

"When did he go down there for the visit?"

"Monique picked him up on Friday morning."

"And did you speak with Kenny while he was down there?"

"On Sunday night. He asked me to come get him since Monique had to stay with her mother."

"So, you went up to Atlanta last weekend?"

"Yes, to get my son."

"Who told you about Mr. Pope?"

"Uh…" Ortega stared at Sean. "I guess Kenny did."

"You guess?"

"Well, it was kind of crazy news."

171

"Sir, where were you last weekend?"

"What does that matter?"

Answering a question with a question—not smart, Ortega.

"Just a question."

"Here all weekend."

"Until Sunday night?"

"Yeah."

"Anyone vouch for that?"

"No…I did get a few calls though."

"What about Kenny's call? When did that come in?"

"Uh…sometime after eight—I think."

"And you drove up immediately—rather than waiting until morning?"

"My son was distraught. I had to go."

Out of the corner of his eye, Sean noticed Chief Vincent standing in the hallway. Vincent motioned for Sean to join him.

"Hang tight for a minute, sir." Sean stood and went over to the chief. "Find something?"

Vincent held up a pair of shoes. "I think there's blood on these."

The chief had gloves on, but Sean didn't. He stared closely at the laces without touching the shoes. "You may be right." He took out his phone and photographed the pair. "Turn them over for me."

Vincent showed him the bottoms of the soles. They were relatively new, and Sean could easily make out the size. He photographed the bottoms as well. "Bag them for me?"

Vincent nodded. "Done."

"Detective?"

Both men turned to see an officer holding a laptop.

From where he stood, Sean could tell it was a Microsoft Surface. His heart rate escalating, he went over and took a close look then nodded at the officer. "Wait here."

Going back to the kitchen, he retrieved his notepad and flipped to the page where he had written the stolen laptop's serial number. Returning to where the officer was standing, Sean gestured at the back of the computer. "Open the stand flap for me."

The back plate was used as a support when the computer sat on a table, and the officer flipped it open to expose the registration information.

Sean compared it to what he had on his pad then looked back at Chief Vincent. "It's the laptop."

"Excellent."

Sean turned back to the officer. "Bag it, please."

"Yes, sir."

"Chief, will you have Mr. Ortega taken back to the precinct for a formal interview. I'll meet you there."

"Copy that."

Sean took the bagged evidence back to his car. For the first time since he got the case, he felt like he had a handle on what had happened. Now to prove it.

ATLANTA HOMICIDE

Metter Police Station
900-942 East Lillian Street
Metter, Georgia
9:15 a.m.

A rambling, single-story structure, the Metter police station had started life as an elementary school, before being repurposed as the police precinct. Remnants of its earlier life were still present, including the school marquee, which had been converted to the precinct's sign.

Sean parked out front. His case hinged on his success in getting Kenny Butler to talk. Every detective knew that they might just get one shot, so they had better make it count. After several minutes formulating his plan, Sean got out of the car, and headed toward the front door.

Inside the main entrance, he found Chief Vincent waiting for him.

"This way." Vincent pointed toward a door. "We have your boy and his father in different interview rooms."

Sean followed the chief through a door and down a hallway. The only things he carried with him were a folder containing the hotel video picture and his cellphone. For what Sean hoped to accomplish, he shouldn't need anything else.

The interview room, even smaller than the seven-foot square box Sean was used to in Atlanta, was nevertheless painted a bright white, giving it the impression of being larger. Kenny Butler sat at a tiny table, wearing blue jeans and a long-sleeved shirt with a rock band logo Sean didn't recognize.

Butler's hands were clenched together in his lap. He appeared even younger in person than he looked in the image from the hotel. Sean forced a smile then set the folder in the middle of the table.

"Kenny, my name is Detective Sparks. I'm with the homicide division of Atlanta PD."

Kenny nodded imperceptibly.

"Would you like something to drink?"

A shake of the head.

Sean closed the door then pulled out the chair opposite Butler, letting the legs drag noisily on the concrete. The folder sat between them undisturbed as Sean made a show of getting out his pen and pad. Butler's eyes were glued to the manila file as if he expected it to explode.

Finally, Sean set a recorder on the table and turned it on. "I'm Detective Sean Sparks with Atlanta PD. I'm in an interview room at Metter police department with Kenny Butler, who is here voluntarily. Correct, Kenny?"

He nodded.

Sean smiled. "Sorry, I need you to say it."

"Yeah."

"The time is 9:25 a.m. on December 24." Sean reached for the folder then acted as if he'd changed his mind. He withdrew his hand. "Got plans for Christmas Eve, Kenny?"

Butler shrugged. "Just hanging out with my dad."

"What about your mom? Are you going to see her?"

"Probably."

"I imagine your grandmother would like to see you, too."

His expression softened instantly. "I hope to get up there tomorrow night."

"You get along well with your grandmother?"

175

"Yeah. She's always been there for my mom and me."

"Nothing like family, is there?"

He shrugged.

"So, Kenny…" Sean kept his voice conversational, casual. "That folder in front of you has a few things in it that are troubling. I'm hoping you can clear up my confusion."

Kenny's eyes remained fixed on the file. "What kinds of things?"

Sean reached out for the folder, slid it ever so slowly across the table toward himself, then lifted the flap so deliberately, he expected it to make a creaking noise. Keeping the contents hidden, he pulled the first photo up and looked at it. If Butler was his killer, he probably feared Sean was about to show him a crime scene photo.

Henderson had often remarked that in his experience, there were two kinds of killers. Those who were proud of what they'd done—and those who didn't want to face their crime. Kenny looked as if he was holding his breath, putting him in the second category.

Finally, Sean dropped the print face up in front of Butler. "Do you recognize who that is?"

Kenny, who finally took a breath, did his best to appear unphased. "Sure, it's me."

"Do you know where that picture came from?"

He shook his head.

"That's the entrance to your room at Comfort Inn. The one in Atlanta where you stayed for the three days leading up to the date of your grandfather's murder."

"Step-grandfather."

"Okay, step-grandfather."

Probably to avoid meeting Sean's gaze, Butler's focus remained on the photo. "So."

Sean took out his phone and pulled up a photo. He held it out for Butler to see.

"You recognize those?"

"Yeah, they're my shoes."

"That's right, and the interesting thing is they're size eight and a half."

"So."

"Well, the person who killed Rodney Pope left some shoeprints. Guess what size."

Butler stared at his hands.

"What's really troubling, though, is your shoes have blood on them."

"Really?"

"That's what it looks like. I'll be having them tested soon."

"Well, I…I…had a nosebleed a few weeks back."

"I see. So the blood would be yours then."

"Yeah."

Sean pulled the phone back and opened a different photo. He held it out to Butler. "Do you recognize this, Kenny?"

This time the boy's eyes widened. "It's a laptop."

"That's right—but not just any laptop. This is the one stolen from your grandmother's house on the night Rodney Pope was murdered."

The boy's top lip quivered. "So?"

"Do I need to tell you where we found it?"

Butler had gone mute.

"Your bedroom. Any idea how it got there?"

No answer.

"Look, Kenny…" Sean set down his phone. "I'm going to tell you what I think led up to Mr. Pope being killed, but before that, I need to read you your Miranda rights. Do you know what those are?"

A quick nod.

"You have the right to remain silent. Anything you say can and will be used against you in a court of law. You have the right to an attorney. If you cannot afford an attorney, one will be provided for you. Do you understand the rights I have just read to you?

"Yes."

"With these rights in mind, do you wish to speak to me?"

"Am I under arrest?"

"No, not as of now."

"I guess."

"Thank you."

Sean closed the folder and scooted his chair closer to Butler. The kid leaned away as far as he could.

Sean sighed. "So, Kenny, here's what I believe happened. Your mother told your dad she was taking you to visit your grandmother. She picked you up on Friday morning then took you to the Comfort Inn and booked you a room. Sometime on Sunday, she arranged for you to be in the alley behind your grandmother's. When she and your grandmother went out to eat that night, you waited for Mr. Pope to take his nightly walk then broke the back glass on the door and let yourself in. You waited for Mr. Pope to come home then attacked him. You had already taken the money in the casino mug and the laptop before the attack even happened."

Sean paused, and tears welled up in the boy's eyes.

"You beat your step-grandfather to death, didn't you, Kenny?"

Butler's slight shoulders shook. "That's not what happened!"

"That's what the evidence is telling me."

"The evidence is wrong!"

Sean scooted a little closer. "Okay then, Kenny, I need you to tell me what really happened."

A long silence followed, with Sean waiting out the boy.

Then, for the first time, Kenny met Sean's gaze. "My mother had nothing to do with it."

"I'm not sure I can believe that."

"It's true. I told my mother I wanted to hang with some friends in the city. She agreed to pay for my hotel room. She didn't know what I was really planning."

"I see. How did you get to the house on Sunday?"

"I walked."

"That's nearly ten miles in the cold."

"I know."

"What happened next?"

"I put tape on the bottom of my shoes and used the baseball bat."

The tape was a new wrinkle. It explained why there was no definition to the shoe prints. Sean wasn't buying that Kenny had come up with that on his own.

"Where's the bat, Kenny?"

"I threw it in the dumpster behind the hotel."

Sean cringed inside. It would be nearly impossible to find the bat now.

He leaned in until he was just inches from Butler and watched the boy's eyes change. They filled with something new— something Sean couldn't put his finger on. *Defiance? Anger? Hatred?*

"Kenny, let's pretend I believe you for a moment. Why did you do it?"

"He made me."

"Who did?"

"Rodney."

"How so?"

"He was so horrible to my gram. He treated her like a slave and was stealing all her money. I couldn't let him do that to her. I love her." The emotion used to spit out the accusations carried with it a sincere belief he spoke the truth.

Sean had little doubt who was responsible for poisoning the kid's mind. "How did you learn about what Mr. Pope was doing?"

Kenny grunted. "I heard about it all the time. Every time mom visited my gram, she would come home upset about what Rodney was doing."

"When you visited your grandmother, did you ever see this treatment for yourself?"

"Rodney wasn't around most of the time I was there."

Sean leaned back from the boy. He had confessed, and in general, his statements were corroborated by the evidence. But the idea that Monique *wasn't* the mastermind seemed ridiculous. Still, if Kenny didn't implicate his mother, it would make it much more difficult to nail her.

Sean stood and opened the door. One of the officers who had assisted in the house search was standing in the hall.

Sean waved him in. "Place Mr. Butler under arrest for murder."

The officer entered the room. "Stand up."

Kenny slowly rose to his feet.

"Turn around."

Moments later, the cuffs had made their signature sound, in this case ending Kenny's freedom. The boy shuffled out the door, leaving Sean in the silent room. Anger raged inside him, battling with a feeling of sadness.

At least for the time being, the anger won out.

Office of Lieutenant Shannon Mitchell
Atlanta Police Headquarters
Homicide Division
226 Peachtree Street SW
Downtown Atlanta
3:45 p.m.

Sean had transported Kenny Butler from Metter to Atlanta in the back of his vehicle. Despite Sean trying several times to get the boy to implicate his mother, Butler was having none of it. He sat silently, his hands cuffed and his mouth curled downward in a grimace until Sean delivered him to the jail.

From there, Sean headed directly to police headquarters. He had given Lieutenant Mitchell a quick update on the phone, but she was waiting to be apprised of all the developments, and Sean wanted her advice on what to do about Monique Butler. He was convinced she was behind the murder, but he only had circumstantial evidence against her, most of which could be explained by the story Kenny had given.

Mitchell caught sight of him from her desk and waved for him to come into the office.

"All right if I grab a coffee, Lieutenant?"

"Of course. I'll get one with you." She rose from her desk and went with him to the coffee machine. "How was the trip back?"

"Not bad, though hopefully, I'm done with road trips for a while."

"I can hardly blame you. You put quite a few miles on your car the last couple days."

"*And* my body."

She grunted. "Don't talk to me about aching bodies. I've got several years and a whole lot more miles on me than you do!"

He laughed. "Yes, ma'am."

They returned to her office, and he closed the door behind him.

Once seated, Mitchell ditched the lighthearted small talk and focused on the serious matter at hand. "Did you get anything new on the trip back?"

Sean shook his head. "He's not giving up his mother."

"What have you got on her?"

"Mostly, her lies. When I showed her the hotel photo, she denied knowing who Kenny was. Instead, she gave me that cock and bull story about helping out a stranded young man."

"I remember. What else?"

"She gave him a ride to Atlanta and paid for the room he stayed in."

"What is Kenny's story about his mother's involvement?"

Sean sighed. "He claims she didn't know of his plan, and he told her he just wanted to spend time with some friends."

Mitchell crossed her arms, leaned back, and turned her face toward the ceiling. Her eyes were closed. Sean sipped his coffee and waited.

His first instinct was to drag Monique Butler down to the station and grill her until she slipped up—but that had its problems. If she walked into the room and asked for a lawyer, he'd be dead in the water, with nothing he could do about it.

He had a second idea, but it was riskier, and he was less sure it would work.

Eventually, his boss opened her eyes and met his gaze. "Without the boy and without any physical evidence, you're going to need a confession."

"That's what I figured."

"How do you propose to get it?"

He shrugged. "Bring her down and grill her?"

Mitchell frowned. "I don't like it. She seems too smart— I think she'll lawyer up."

"That's my thought, too. I had another idea…"

She laid her head to one side. "Good. What is it?"

"Talk to her at the Popes' house, in front of her mother."

Mitchell's eyebrows arched upward. "Your reasoning?"

"Twofold. First, more comfortable surroundings for Butler."

"Less likely to lawyer up, is that it?"

"Yeah."

"Okay. What's the other?"

"Lots of folks have a hard time lying in front of their mother. If I can get Mrs. Pope questioning her daughter, maybe Monique will crack."

"How do you get it on tape?"

"I have an idea for that, too."

She stared at him for a moment then rocked forward in her chair. "I like it."

His second gold star on this case. He only hoped it worked out like he planned, or instead of hanging a gold star around his neck, she might choke him with it.

He stood. "I'm hoping I can catch them at home tonight."

"Perfect. Good luck."

"Thank you."

He returned to his desk and dialed Felicity Pope.

"Hello?"

"Mrs. Pope, it's Detective Sparks."

"Hello, Detective."

"Is Monique with you?"

"Yes. We're spending Christmas Eve together. Would you like to talk to her?"

"Actually... Would it be too much trouble if I came by?"

"Tonight?"

"Yes, ma'am. I have news, and I'd really like to share it with you in person."

"Then by all means."

Mrs. Pope's willingness to have him over indicated to Sean that she wasn't afraid of what he might say—the exact reason he'd called her and not Monique.

"Great. I'll be there soon."
"See you then."
He hung up.
Showtime, Sean, old boy.

Home of Rodney and Felicity Pope
2905 Renfro Drive NW
Collier Heights Neighborhood
West Atlanta
5:45 p.m.

Sean parked and got out. The northwest wind whipped at his back as he waited for the patrol car to arrive.

Moments later, Officer Tom Bradley pulled up next to Sean's car and stopped, rolling down his window. "You requested I meet you here?"

Sean nodded. "I want you to go inside with me. I'll be conducting an interview, and I need a support officer but don't want to raise their suspicion about what I'm there for. The women should remember you, and hopefully, they'll be less wary of why you're present."

"Okay, if you say so."

"You have a body cam on?"

"I do."

"Make sure it's running before we enter. Once inside, position yourself so the lens can cover the whole room. Appear casual and follow my lead."

"Sounds good."

185

"Let's go."

With a small briefcase under one arm and Bradley in tow, Sean approached Mrs. Pope's front door.

Monique Butler greeted them or, more accurately, blocked their entrance to the house. Her face reflected nothing resembling a welcome. "A little unusual to come by on Christmas Eve, isn't it, Detective?"

"Yes, ma'am. I'm afraid this couldn't wait."

"I trust it won't take long."

"I hope not."

She glared at Bradley. "Why the police escort?"

"You remember Officer Bradley, don't you? He responded to your 9-1-1 call."

"Oh, yes."

"He wanted to be present when I delivered my news."

Butler hesitated, her gaze fixed on the officer, likely convinced there was no way of delaying them further. "You'd better come in then."

They followed her into the entryway.

Sean smiled at Mrs. Pope. "Thank you for letting us intrude."

She returned the smile, though it was muted. "It's fine. Monique and I were just about to have some coffee. Would you care to join us?"

"No, thank you."

A flash of recognition crossed her face. "Officer Bradley, correct?"

"Yes, ma'am. Good evening."

"How about you? Coffee?"

"No, but thank you, ma'am."

Mrs. Pope gestured toward a pair of armchairs. "Please, make yourselves at home."

Sean accepted the offer, but Bradley deferred. "I've been sitting in the patrol car all day. I hope you don't mine if I stand."

"However you're most comfortable."

Monique moved over by the couch and joined her mother opposite Sean. He laid the briefcase on the coffee table in front of him and opened it. The lid swung up and blocked the women from seeing what was inside.

Sean focused his attention on Mrs. Pope, but he watched Butler out of the corner of his eye.

"Mrs. Pope, I wanted to speak with you this evening because we've had a break in the case."

"Oh?"

"We've arrested your husband's killer."

Felicity Pope's eyes welled up. "Really?" She looked at her daughter. "You hear that, Monique? They caught him."

Sean watched the two women, and their reactions told him everything he needed to know. Pope was emotional, even thrilled. Butler looked grim.

Monique nearly snarled her response. "I heard, Mom. That's something, isn't it?"

Sean turned directly to Butler. "I have good news for you."

"Oh?"

Sean lifted the laptop, still in the evidence bag, out of the briefcase. "We found your laptop."

"Wow."

187

He held it out to Butler, but she didn't reach for it. He held it in the air for a second longer then laid it on the table next to the briefcase.

Her pupils were pinpoints as it appeared panic was setting in. "Are you sure it's mine?"

"Yes, ma'am. The serial number matched."

Mrs. Pope gushed, apparently oblivious to her daughter's distress. "That's wonderful. But who killed my husband?"

Sean reached into the briefcase again, this time coming out with the hotel photo. "This man."

Both women saw the photo at the same time. Monique's face was frozen in a combination of shock and horror.

Mrs. Pope appeared confused. "I don't understand. That's Kenny."

"Yes, ma'am." Sean was speaking to Pope but his attention was focused on Butler. "I'm afraid your grandson is the one who killed Rodney Pope."

"But...but that's impossible. Kenny would never do something like that!" She turned to her daughter. "Monique, tell him he's mistaken."

Butler had locked eyes with Sean, hate radiating from her gaze. "It's ridiculous. Kenny is a good boy."

Without breaking eye contact, Sean lifted the Mastercard statement out of the case and held it up.

"This statement says that you, Miss Butler, paid for the room your son stayed in prior to the murder."

She stared at him, ignoring the paper, silent.

"Then Sunday night, you gave your son the signal to go ahead with the plan."

"I did no such thing. Yes, I rented him a room, but it was so he could hang out with his friends."

188

Sean laid the paper on the laptop. "That's what Kenny said...at first."

Butler's fists had clenched, and every muscle in her face had gone rigid. "At first?"

"That's right, until I told him how you denied knowing who he was. That you just helped out a stranger. At that point, he realized you were going to let him hang for the murder alone."

Felicity Pope had gone mute. Her gaze tracked back and forth from Sean to her daughter, as if watching a tennis match with deadly stakes.

Monique's voice lowered to a hiss. "*If* Kenny did do this, *he* took it upon himself."

At that moment, Sean wanted to reach across the table and choke her. He realized his fists were now clenched.

Just inches away sat a mother who would crucify her flesh and blood to save her skin—just about the most vile thing he could think of. Sean pushed the emotion aside and focused on his task.

"You and I both know that's not the truth." Sean barely recognized his voice. His words flowed out with controlled venom. "Kenny told me everything. How you constantly complained that Mr. Pope treated your mother badly—even claimed he abused her. How Mr. Pope acted as if she was a slave and only wanted her money. He poured it all out."

Felicity stared at her daughter. "Is that true?"

Monique stared at Sean, rage surging up inside her, oozing from every pore.

Her mother pushed. "Monique, it's not, is it?"

Monique didn't respond.

"*Monique*! I'm talking to you!"

189

Butler ripped her stare away from Sean and turned on her mother. "What was I supposed to do? Let him take our money! Let him ruin our lives?"

Tears welled up in Felicity's eyes. "What are you talking about?"

"The house, our savings."

"*Our* money? *Our* savings? None of that belonged to you!" Felicity was screaming now. "You ruined my grandson's life over money?"

Butler stared at her mother, seemingly unable to come up with an answer.

Sean's anger had turned to relief. He had his confession.

Looking up at Bradley, he gestured at Monique and nodded.

The officer came into the room and stood behind her. "Stand up, please."

Butler looked at him, confusion on her face. "Why?"

"Just stand up, please."

She rose to her feet.

Sean waited until she was cuffed. "Monique Butler, you are under arrest for conspiracy to commit murder. Officer Bradley will read you your rights and escort you downtown."

Bradley led Butler outside.

Felicity had her face buried in her hands, and sobs filled the little room.

"I'm sorry, Mrs. Pope."

Regardless of the state of Felicity and Rodney Pope's relationship, Sean believed she never wanted her husband killed. Now, in a cruel twist, she had to face the fact that the people she loved most had done it. The series of events will be the cause of unimaginable pain.

190

He slowly put everything away in the briefcase and waited for the woman to calm down. After more than thirty minutes, she wiped at her face and looked up at him.

"What will happen to Kenny?"

He shrugged. "I don't know exactly. There's no doubt he's guilty of murder, but there were extenuating circumstances involving your daughter. It's out of my hands at this point."

She nodded.

"I'm so sorry." Sean swallowed hard. "Is there someone I can call for you?"

She shook her head. "I'll call Andre later."

Sean was relieved to hear she would reach out to Mr. Gordon. Maybe he could help get her through this. "Again, I'm very sorry for your loss." He got to his feet.

"Detective?"

"Ma'am."

"Can I see my grandson?"

He hesitated but only for a moment. "Yes, ma'am. I'll take you to him."

Atlanta Police Headquarters
Homicide Division
226 Peachtree Street SW
Downtown Atlanta
8:15 p.m.

Sean stood in the observation room watching Felicity Pope and Kenny Butler hug. Tears flowed from both as

191

Kenny apologized repeatedly while his grandmother told him she didn't blame him.

From the interaction, it was clear that Felicity held her daughter responsible for the situation her grandson was in. While it wasn't completely true, Sean hoped the court would see things in a similar way. Maybe Kenny Butler's life might still come to something constructive one day.

Sean certainly agreed with the idea that Kenny never would have committed such a heinous act without his mother's influence. Monique Butler was the real sociopath in the family. He hoped they'd lock her up somewhere and throw away the key.

He had made the unusual decision to pull Kenny from his cell and have him brought to an interview room where he could meet with his grandmother. Sean owed Mrs. Pope that much. After all, he'd made her an unwitting participant in extracting a confession from her daughter.

If it started her down the path to some sort of closure, then he'd worry about protocol later. He glanced at his watch then left the observation room. A jailer stood outside the interview room, waiting to return Kenny to the lock-up.

He'd promised Mrs. Pope a half hour, and time was growing short. Sean tapped lightly on the door then pushed it open. Two sets of swollen eyes looked up at him.

"It's time."

Felicity nodded and turned to Kenny. She took his head in her hands and locked eyes with him.

"Be strong. I'm going to get you help—okay?"

"Yes, Gram."

"And don't forget I love you. Nothing has changed that."

"I love you, too."

She kissed his forehead and then released him. Kenny stood for the jailer to put the cuffs back on him.

When Kenny was gone, Felicity looked up at Sean. "Thank you."

"You're welcome. Officer Bradley is waiting to take you home."

****

After nearly two hours of paperwork, Sean was finally ready to call it a day. He'd done it. Closed his first case as a lead—solo lead, at that—and despite the circumstances, his heart was filled with a combined sense of satisfaction and redemption.

His hunches had panned out and he'd got the right answers. He checked the time—10:45. Not too late to send a text to Mariah.

Still awake?

Yes.

Closed the case.

Awesome. Congrats!

Can I still come by?

Mom and Dad are in bed, but I'd love to see you.

193

Be there soon.

☺

Home of the Coopers
Buckhead Village Neighborhood
North of Downtown
11:30 p.m.

Sean had run by his apartment on the way. When he finally arrived, Mariah greeted him in a red Christmas sweater with a green LED tree that twinkled. He laughed and kissed her.

"Sorry for the late arrival."

"I understand. I'm just glad you could get away."

She led him into the living room where two glasses of wine waited. They sat on the couch together, and she handed him a glass then raised her own.

"To solving your first case."

They clinked glasses and drank. Strawberry wine, her favorite.

"I wanted to keep our tradition of being together when Christmas morning arrived."

"I'm so happy you could make it."

They snuggled on the couch, and he relished in her warmth. It was more than the sweater and her delicate touch;

this was his safe space. Next to her, the darkness of his work was pushed away, and the joy of being with her took over.

He watched the clock sitting on the fireplace mantel until it chimed midnight. Pushing himself up to a sitting position, he looked back at her.

"Well, it's Christmas morning, so I guess I can give you your present."

Her eyes shimmered with anticipation. "I can't wait."

A small box magically appeared in his hand, which he held out to her. "Here."

She gasped then reached out with two hands to take it. Slowly, she lifted the lid. "Oh, it's beautiful."

"I wanted to get you something really special this year."

A tinge of confusion crossed her face. "But, Sean, this is an engagement ring."

"I know. Mariah Cooper, will you marry me?"

Her eyes welled over, and she flung herself against him, wrapping her arms around his neck. "Oh, Sean!"

He held her tight. "I'll take that as a yes."

She pushed back and locked eyes with him. "It is definitely a yes."

"Good, because…"

"Because what?"

He shrugged. "I was worried my work and not being around for the last week, well…it may have made you question…"

"Sean Sparks, let me tell you something. The man I fell in love with is someone who wants to make a difference and who cares deeply about people. If being a detective is how you do that, then I'm proud to be your partner in that life."

He took the ring out of the box and placed it on her finger. "Merry Christmas."

She glowed, staring at the ring. "You want your present?"

"I already got it. My secondary gift can wait till morning."

They snuggled up again, and Sean promptly passed out.

<u>Monday, December 25</u>

<u>Christmas Day</u>

Home of Janine Evans
Myrtle Street NE
Midtown Atlanta
10:30 a.m.

Mariah watched Sean get out of the car. They had spent Christmas morning with her parents, and during that time, Sean had received two text messages. He'd shared them both with her. The first was from his Lieutenant.

Congratulations on closing the case, Sean.
Solid work.
Merry Christmas. Shannon.

The second had come from Lance Henderson.

Mitchell filled me in. Great job, Rook.
Like I said—you're good.
Merry Christmas. Lance.

After breakfast and presents, Sean said he had an errand to run that was related to work, but this time, he wanted her to go. She happily agreed.

It had been her practice not to ask anything other than general questions about his job. She wanted to be the person—and their home to be the place—he went to when he needed to get away from the pressures of his work. So when he asked her to go along, it meant this trip was special to him, and he wanted her there.

All morning, Sean had seemed different. Nothing dramatic and not tied to them getting engaged, but something else—something inside. As she watched him walk up the stairs leading from the street to the small house where they'd stopped, it finally came to her.

Peace—inner peace. Solving his first case seemed to have solidified the direction and purpose of his life. He hadn't said so directly, but she could feel it.

The house Sean approached was one of the few without Christmas decorations—no lights, no wreath, and no tree in the window. He rang the bell and waited. Within a few moments, a woman in a pink bathrobe came to the door.

Sean spoke to her, and though Mariah couldn't hear the words, she could see the impact. The woman's hand went to her mouth, then she stepped forward and hugged Sean. When she stepped back, tears were streaming down her face. The woman's lips mouthed the words, *Thank you.*

She turned and went back inside.

Sean came down the steps and got back into the car. He had tears in his eyes.

She reached out and took his hand. "Who was that?"

"Rodney Pope's daughter."

"You told her who killed her father?"

"Yes. I promised her I would do my best to find out. I wanted to deliver on that."

198

She kissed the back of his hand. "I love you, Mr. Sparks"

"Love you more, future Mrs. Sparks."

"Not possible."

He smiled at her. "I believe this time, you might be right."

Author's Note

Number 9 in the series is done, and number 10 is planned for 2020. The series has been enjoyable for me to write, and visiting new cities has been an interesting experience. Atlanta is filled with fascinating and historical venues, some of which I tried to feature in the book.

I hope that you, the readers, find this story a worthy

ATLANTA HOMICIDE

inclusion to *THE CITY MURDERS* series. After all, it's because of your reviews and letters that we have the confidence to continue on this writing journey.

God Bless,
      John & Bev
      I John 1:9

Cover by Beverly Dalglish
Edited by Jill Noelle-Noble
Proofreading by Robert Toohey

Made in the USA
Columbia, SC
29 June 2020